DEATH VALLEY

A THRILLER

J.F. PENN

Death Valley. A Thriller
Copyright © J.F. Penn (2025).

Special Edition Hardback ISBN: 978-1-915425-87-4
Paperback ISBN: 978-1-915425-88-1
Large Print ISBN: 978-1-915425-89-8
Ebook ISBN: 978-1-915425-90-4
Audiobook ISBN: 978-1-915425-91-1

Requests to publish work from this book should be
sent to: joanna@JFPenn.com

Cover and interior images generated by J.F. Penn on DALLE and Midjourney with commercial license

Cover and Interior Design: JD Smith Design

Published by Curl Up Press

www.CurlUpPress.com

"Everything that ever happened to me that was important happened in the desert."

—Michael Ondaatje, *The English Patient*

"Maybe there is a beast… maybe it's only us."

—William Golding, *Lord of the Flies*

CHAPTER 1

As dawn crept across Death Valley's Badwater Basin, the first rays of sun caught the crystalline salt flats like the reflection of a knife blade.

Casey Thornton sat alone on the worn steps of the observatory on a ridge above the basin, one knee pulled up to her chest, watching light spill over the lowest point in North America. The vast salt pan stretched below her like a twisted mirror, its surface fractured into endless geometric patterns. In the growing light, the salt crystals sparkled and shadows pooled in the fractures.

It was quiet and still.

No birdsong, no rustling leaves. No burble of gentle water streaming over the rocks. None of the familiar sounds she'd grown up with in England's green and rainy southwest hills. Just the whisper of her breathing and the occasional soft ping of the observatory's metal walls expanding in the rapidly warming air.

Casey came here every morning to savor these moments of perfect solitude when the desert belonged to no one, where she could imagine a past before humans walked here, and a future with nothing left but desert.

The emptiness gave her perspective. In the face of such majesty, she was nothing upon the face of the earth. Her past mistakes, however terrible, were so slight as to be insignificant. She could make it through one more day.

She took a deep breath.

It was late spring and, while the air was still cool, by mid-morning the heat would be brutal, especially out there on the salt flats. Her water bottle, slick with condensation, dripped onto the step beside her and Casey was aware of every precious drop of moisture. Back home, the English complained incessantly about the rain, but after living in Death Valley for even a brief few months, she would never take the cool damp weather for granted again.

A shadow passed overhead, and Casey tilted her face up, squinting against the strengthening sunlight.

A golden eagle rode the morning thermal, its wingspan casting a dark cross against the sky, now streaked with shades of pink and coral. She tracked the bird's lazy circles as it caught another updraft, soaring higher without apparent effort.

It was free. Untethered. With no regrets over what it had killed.

If only she could channel that strength.

The eagle banked sharply, angling toward the deep shadows of Coffin Peak. Casey watched until it disappeared, just another speck of life making its way in this harshest of environments.

She looked across the salt flats to where the pastel bands of mineral deposits painted the foothills in streaks of rust red, sulfur yellow, and a pale green that shifted into almost psychedelic shades under a certain light. So different to the Mendip Hills near her home, where everything was a muted variation of emerald and moss, or slate gray and earthy brown.

To the east, the Amargosa Range caught the full force of sunrise, its peaks glowing amber against a sky that deepened from pearl to turquoise with each passing minute.

Closer in, by the edge of the salt pan, a stand of creosote bushes dotted the alluvial fan, their leaves gleaming with oil that filled the warming air with a sharp, clean scent. The bushes were scattered far apart, each one claiming its territory of precious water, unlike the crowded hedgerows and tangled woodland back home.

Everything about this landscape was different to England — its scale, its severity, its sublime indifference to human presence. Primeval forces had shaped the ground beneath her feet, with the movement of ancient lake beds, tectonic upheaval, and millions of years of wind and sun and salt.

In Somerset, centuries of human habitation had shaped every hill and dale, softened by sheep grazing and crisscrossed by ancient stone walls. But here, despite generations of humans struggling to tame it, Death Valley remained terrifyingly wild.

The perfect escape.

Casey inhaled deeply, tasting dust and minerals on her tongue. Out here, she could push away the memories more easily, and the echoing screams in that cave back in Somerset felt distant, almost unreal. The constricting stone walls that pressed in, stealing the air from her lungs, had no power in this vast, open space. Here, the horizon stretched on forever, and the sky was an endless canopy of light. Here, she could breathe.

The wind stirred, hot already, though the sun had barely cleared the mountains. It whispered across the salt pan, raising tiny dust devils that danced briefly before dissolving. Casey watched them spin themselves into nothing, remembering her grandmother's warning about spirits of the wild places. About how they wouldn't recognize her. She was not of this land.

She had called Casey mad for taking this job, for leaving behind everything familiar to work in a godforsaken desert with a terrifying promise in its name.

But that was exactly why Casey had come.

To find a place so vast and empty that its immensity would dwarf her ghosts. A place where she could rebuild herself in the stark light of day, far from the underground darkness that still haunted her dreams, and the people of the small Somerset village who still saw her as she had been in those dark days after the accident.

The wind gusted stronger, carrying the mineral scents of salt and sunbaked rock and something herbal — sage, maybe, from the scrubland below. Natural smells, clean and sharp, so different from the damp earth and moss she'd grown up with.

Casey glanced at her watch.

It was almost time to transform into the capable adventure guide, projecting confidence and competence and always wearing a friendly smile. Americans loved a British accent, and she loved the advantage it gave her, especially with the wealthy guests who came out here to experience a taste of the wilderness, even as they were protected from its dangers in every way.

Casey turned and looked down the other side of the ridge at the award-winning Desert Sanctuary complex below, its sweeping curves of glass and reclaimed wood artfully mirroring the undulating lines of the dunes, shaped by the relentless wind and the baking heat of the sun.

While the desert stretched vast and unforgiving in every direction, the Sanctuary offered an oasis of almost impossible luxury, certified as ecologically net zero to assuage any lingering guilt over its extravagance.

Private villas and suites dotted the property, some with infinity pools that seemed to merge with the desert beyond. The water sparkled in the morning light, so much precious moisture left to evaporate under the desert sun. But tasteful excess was all part of the expectation of the guests — and the latest batch would soon be arriving.

Desert style gardens surrounded the villas, giving the guests a sense of privacy while also making them feel as if they were actually out in the wild. Tall Joshua trees stood like sentries along curved pathways, while beds of desert marigolds and purple verbena added splashes of color that nature would never have allowed to congregate so densely. An intricate drip irrigation system kept the plants alive, all to maintain the illusion of perfectly controlled wilderness.

At the heart of it all rose the main Sanctuary building, crowned by its architecturally award-winning glass dome. The grand dining room and bar — on a raised level within — offered panoramic views of the desert, allowing guests to observe the harsh landscape while enjoying climate-controlled comfort.

All too soon the space would be filled with the murmur of voices and the pop of champagne corks. But for now, the dome caught the morning light — a giant lens focusing the sun's growing strength.

Casey looked out toward the line of dune buggies parked at the front of the adventure garage, its wide door open to the morning breeze. She'd already checked that all were cleaned and fueled for the day ahead before driving one of them up the ridge to the observatory.

She ran through her mental checklist: Emergency supplies in each vehicle. Satellite phones charged, GPS units programmed with safe routes and danger zones clearly marked. The desert didn't forgive mistakes, and she refused to let anything happen to her charges, no matter how reckless they might be with their own safety.

She'd learned that the hard way.

One moment of distraction, one failure to double-check equipment, and—

The drone of aircraft engines shattered the morning stillness and forced her out of the spiral into darker thoughts.

Casey looked to the horizon and spotted the small plane,

a white speck against the now vast blue canvas of sky, making its final approach across the salt pans towards the Sanctuary.

There would be several planes arriving this morning with the guests for the week ahead, each expecting the highest standards of service as well as memorable experiences they couldn't get anywhere else.

Casey pushed herself up from the observatory steps, brushing dust from her cargo pants. Time to become the professional they all expected.

She ran her fingers through her short dark hair, cropped close to her neck — a practical style, so different from the long waves she'd worn back in England. The desert encouraged her to strip away anything unnecessary, and she had wanted to transform, to be almost unrecognizable to those who knew her back home. She worked out in the hotel's gym as often as she could, and she kept her calorie intake to the minimum.

Some might say she punished her body for its betrayal, but Casey only wanted to become someone different. Someone harder.

Just in case.

She did a quick inventory of her gear as she strode toward the dune buggy, its reinforced roll cage gleaming in the strengthening sun.

Radio clipped to her belt, fully charged. First aid kit secured behind the passenger seat, more comprehensive than even the resort required. Supplies for snake bites, heat exhaustion, and the countless other ways the desert could kill. Emergency water cached in insulated containers. Satellite phone. Rescue blankets. Flare gun. Things she hoped she would never need.

Casey swung into the driver's seat, adjusted her sunglasses, and buckled the five-point harness. The engine roared to life with a satisfying growl that echoed off the cliff face.

She took a moment to check the gauges. Fuel, oil pressure, temperature. All optimal. Casey eased the buggy into gear and began the descent along the narrow track that switch-backed down the cliff face.

The path was treacherous, loose scree shifting under the tires as she navigated the hairpin turns. One mistake, one moment of inattention, and gravity would claim them both. But Casey knew every inch of this trail and let the buggy's weight work with her rather than fighting it, enjoying the last minutes of alone time.

The small plane drew closer, heading toward the private airstrip at one side of the hotel.

Several of the welcome staff had already driven golf carts to the edge of the runway, ready to take the bags and drive the guests into the shade.

As the plane descended, Casey could almost feel the weight of expectation pressing down. The demands, the secrets, the complications that always came with guests wealthy enough to afford this luxurious paradise.

The morning's peace retreated like a mirage, leaving behind the stark reality of what the Sanctuary truly was: A stage set where the ultra-rich could play at adventure. A desert experience with none of the danger of this brutal landscape. A carefully crafted illusion created by Casey and her fellow workers. It was time to maintain that illusion for the next set of guests.

CHAPTER 2

CASEY STEERED THE DUNE buggy into its designated spot as the morning's gentle warmth evolved into the fierce heat that Death Valley was infamous for. She could feel it radiating from the asphalt of the parking area and see it shimmering above the dark surface like invisible flames.

The staff entrance was marked only by a discreet keypad, its brushed metal housing already hot to the touch. Casey punched in her code and pulled open the heavy door, bracing herself for the transition.

The artificial cold hit her like a physical wall, shocking her desert-warmed skin and making her catch her breath. Goosebumps rose on her arms as she walked into the carefully manufactured environment of the Sanctuary.

Time to put on her game face.

She straightened her shoulders, adjusted her name badge, checked her reflection in the brushed steel wall. The woman who looked back was a professional, someone who knew what she was doing. Someone who could be trusted with the lives of others.

"Buenos días, Casey." Manuel from maintenance nodded as he passed, pushing a cart of tools. "AC's running high today. Ms. Jensen's orders. Guests coming in from the heat. You know how it is."

"Thanks for the warning." She managed a smile, though she never understood the American obsession with arctic indoor temperatures. Yet another artificial extreme in this place of natural ones.

She quickened her pace and hurried through the high-ceilinged corridors and into the grand atrium.

The space opened up before her, a soaring cathedral of glass and steel that brought the desert inside while keeping its deadly touch at bay. Morning light poured through the vast windows, creating shifting patterns on the polished stone floor.

The walls on either side featured artwork created by local Timbisha Shoshone artists, installations that told stories of the valley.

The largest piece dominated the wall behind the reception desk, a striking mixed-media work that depicted the desert's seasons of feast and famine. Coyote featured prominently, as he did in many Timbisha tales, his figure simultaneously playful and menacing. The piece incorporated real desert sand and minerals, their colors shifting as the morning light played across the surface.

Beneath the artwork, a small plaque carried the words of the artist: 'The desert does not care for your wealth or status. It will transform you, or it will destroy you. The choice is not yours to make.'

Casey knew the words by heart, having read them every morning for the few months she'd been here, finding in them a hope for her own transformation.

The other pieces were equally powerful. Beadwork that captured the shimmer of heat waves over salt flats, woven sculptures that traced the path of flash floods through narrow canyons, and painted stories of those who had wandered into the valley unprepared and never returned. Beauty and danger, the desert's ever-present dichotomy.

The plane taxied to a halt outside, and the staff assembled

in their usual formation, a carefully choreographed arrangement designed to project both efficiency and welcome. Everyone had been briefed on the guests to serve them better in the days ahead and make their experience an extraordinary one.

Casey headed over to the gathering staff and took her position among the other adventure guides.

Security chief Jack Abrams stood slightly apart from the group, in a place where he could survey both the entrance and the bank of security monitors partially hidden behind a decorative screen.

Even in the resort's sand-toned uniform, Jack radiated military precision. His shirt was pressed knife-sharp, his boots gleaming despite the desert dust that coated everything by day's end. A radio earpiece curled around his right ear, and his eyes strayed to the tactical watch on his wrist, checking the time with mechanical regularity. Casey had seen him do the same thing during staff meetings, counting the seconds, probably calculating escape routes and response times in his head.

His gaze flicked up to the monitors now, tracking movement with predatory focus. A maintenance golf cart crossing the grounds. A housekeeper restocking towels by the central pool. A lizard skittering across one of the external cameras. He cataloged each detail, his expression unchanging except for the slight narrowing of his eyes when he noticed Casey watching him.

"Eyes front," he muttered, just loud enough for her to hear. "Try to look professional for once."

Casey bit back a retort. No point engaging.

She and Jack were like matter and antimatter, their worldviews so opposed that any contact only led to explosion. She'd learned that the hard way in her first staff meeting, when his rant about survival of the fittest had nearly driven her to violence.

The click of heels on marble announced Tara Jensen's arrival before she appeared.

The owner of the Sanctuary moved like royalty, her slim figure draped in a sand-colored silk dress that somehow remained unwrinkled. Her dark skin seemed to glow in the morning light, and her perfectly styled hair defied both gravity and the humidity-destroying air conditioning.

Her usual subtle makeup concealed any hint of fatigue, but Casey knew Tara would have been up since dawn, reviewing staff reports, double-checking the most luxurious suites, and ensuring her domain ran with clockwork precision. While other resort owners might trust such details to their employees, Tara controlled every inch of the Desert Sanctuary.

"Places, everyone." Tara's voice carried without her having to raise it. She moved down the line of staff, adjusting a name badge here, straightening a collar there.

She reached Casey, pausing to assess her appearance.

Casey fought the urge to smooth her hair again. Next to Tara's perfection, everyone else looked slightly disheveled.

Tara smiled. "Play up your British accent with Mr. Carver-Scott, won't you? He has a weakness for *Downton Abbey*."

Casey stifled an eye roll at the stereotype and nodded. "Of course."

The main doors whispered open, bringing a blast of desert heat and the sound of voices as staff accompanied the guests inside.

Celebrity chef Rafael Ortiz entered first, his trademark red bandana bright against his tanned skin. He was smaller in person than he appeared in his YouTube videos, but he carried himself with the confident swagger of someone used to being watched. A two-person camera crew trailed behind him, capturing shots from different angles.

"Welcome to the Sanctuary." Tara glided forward, hand extended. "We're honored to have you with us."

"The honor's all mine." Rafael gestured to his camera-men. "Mind if we get some B-roll? The lighting in here is incredible."

"Of course." Tara's smile didn't waver, though Casey saw her stiffen slightly. "But please respect our other guests' privacy and keep them out of shot."

Rafael was already wandering toward the artwork, his crew tracking his movement. "This place is wild, guys," he addressed the camera, his on-screen persona clicking into place like a mask. "Check out this indigenous art. These local people are the real heart of the desert and we'll be eating just like them soon enough."

Casey had watched a couple of Rafael's videos, all machismo and bloodlust as he slaughtered endangered species for views in exotic locations around the world.

Jack shifted position, moving to keep Rafael and his cameras in clear view. The chef's reputation for outrageous stunts clearly hadn't escaped the security chief's notice.

Casey recalled the incident that had made Rafael head-line news. He'd broken into a protected wildlife sanctuary to hunt and eat a critically endangered bird. The video had gone viral, earning him millions of views and a hefty fine that he'd laughed off as a business expense.

"The private kitchen is ready for Rafael's special require-ments," Tara murmured to her staff. "He'll be preparing the centerpiece for the banquet, so please, make no comment on his activities. We're here to facilitate, not judge."

Casey glanced over at the resort's ecological sustain-ability pledge emblazoned on a plaque behind reception. How much of it would survive contact with Rafael's brand of shock entertainment?

She kept her face neutral, professional. After all, wasn't she also playing a part? The capable guide, dependable and trustworthy, with no hint of her past mistakes showing through the facade.

The next guest through the door was more subdued. Barclay Turner slipped through like someone used to going unnoticed, his leather messenger bag clutched against his chest like a shield.

The bag was expensive but well-worn, with scratches and scuffs, and he had the slightly unkempt look of someone who forgot to check his appearance in mirrors. He scanned the atrium, taking in every detail with a hungry gaze that Casey recognized from other writers who'd stayed at the Sanctuary. They were always searching for material to turn reality into fiction and transform people into characters. Magpies of a kind, looking for the next shiny object to use in their work.

Barclay paused in front of the Timbisha artwork, his head tilted to one side.

"Mr. Turner" — Tara approached him with a practiced smile — "we're delighted to have you with us. I understand you're researching the area for a new book?"

"Yes, yes." He barely looked at her, still lost in the painting. "Fascinating region. So many lost stories. So many... buried secrets."

A ripple of movement drew Casey's attention to the doors as Grace Lin entered.

The social media influencer was known for her designer fashion and luxury travel videos, but her accounts had been quiet recently. Today she wore loose hemp clothing in natural beige, her face bare of makeup. She carried a canvas tote bag emblazoned with environmental slogans, and her phone remained out of sight.

Perhaps she was trying something new, but clearly, the influencer side of her could not be contained. As Grace accepted a welcome glass of champagne, she assessed the angles of the space, the way the light fell, and her fingers kept darting to her shoulder bag, actively resisting the urge to pull out a phone. Casey suspected it wouldn't stay hidden for long. This place was designed to be shareable and provoke social media envy.

"Welcome, Ms. Lin." Tara's tone was smooth as ever. "I understand your father is interested in learning more about our sustainability initiatives."

"Is he?" Grace's voice was cool. "Funny, since his companies are responsible for half the luxury developments currently destroying the Mojave desert ecosystem."

Tara's smile didn't waver, but Casey noticed a slight tightening around her eyes. Before she could respond, the doors opened again.

Maxwell Carver-Scott entered like he owned the place — which, given the size of his reservation deposit, he practically did.

The tech billionaire moved with the contained energy of someone used to bending the world to his will. His silver hair was expertly styled to look casually tousled, and his linen suit probably cost more than Casey made in a month.

"Welcome to the Desert Sanctuary." Tara stepped forward, but Maxwell was already scanning the staff line-up with the air of a man reviewing troops.

Behind him came his wife Simone, one hand resting protectively on their daughter Isla's shoulder. Simone was stunning in that seemingly effortless way that only the very wealthy could maintain. Every hair perfectly in place, her makeup flawless, and her coral silk dress cut with the kind of precision that announced its cost without needing a label.

Isla bounced beside her, all long limbs and barely contained energy, her eyes wide with excitement at a new place.

Casey saw the exact moment Simone noticed Jack.

Her step faltered, and something flickered across her perfect features. Recognition, surprise, and something else. Fear? Desire? It was gone too quickly to read.

Jack's reaction was more controlled, but there was a sudden tension in his shoulders and he clenched one fist.

Their eyes met for a fraction of a second before both looked away, their faces settling into careful masks of indifference.

But Casey could see the taut control remain in Jack's posture and the razor-sharp anger he kept barely hidden under security protocol. She had felt the keen edge of it in last week's staff meeting.

Casey had been arguing for additional safety precautions on the hiking trails, especially for younger guests like Isla.

"They're paying for an *authentic* desert experience." Jack's tone dripped with contempt. "They're not to be coddled by your European bleeding-heart safety standards."

"They're paying to *survive* their authentic desert experience," Casey shot back. "Or did you skip the chapter on duty of care in your security manual?"

"Survival isn't a team sport, Thornton. The desert doesn't care about your socialist ideals of protecting the weak. Out here, it's adapt or die."

"Right, because letting children get heat stroke is great for business. Do you actually believe this macho prepper bullshit, or is it just your personality substitute?"

The argument had ended with both of them called into Tara's office for a lecture on professional behavior. But watching Jack now, the way he tracked Simone's movement across the atrium, Casey wondered what secrets their head of security kept hidden behind his survival-of-the-fittest facade.

Staff circulated with trays of fresh juice and champagne.

Oblivious to the tensions, Maxwell chose a green smoothie, while Simone's hand trembled slightly as she lifted a champagne flute to her perfectly lipsticked mouth.

Grace had left her champagne, untouched, on a low table, her attention fixed on the desert visible through the high windows.

Rafael grabbed glasses of juice and champagne from a staff member, swigging both as he played to his cameras with exaggerated appreciation.

Tara assembled the guests in the center of the atrium,

where the morning sun created a natural spotlight on the reclaimed wooden steps.

Her welcome speech was a masterpiece of subtle flattery and exclusive promise, each word carefully chosen to stroke egos while establishing the resort's prestige.

"You are among the select few to experience the Desert Sanctuary, and I know you will uniquely appreciate all we offer here. Not just luxury, but communion with one of the world's most extraordinary landscapes."

Rafael's camera crew adjusted their angles to catch both him and Tara in the same frame, while Grace's studied indifference couldn't quite hide her influencer's instinct to document everything. Barclay retreated to the periphery, scribbling in a notebook.

As Tara concluded her speech, the staff members responsible for various aspects of the resort stepped forward to introduce themselves and offer options for both relaxation and entertainment.

When her turn came, Casey smiled in welcome. "I'm Casey Thornton, head of the adventure team. I'll be taking a tour of the property by dune buggy. It's the best way to appreciate the scale and beauty of our little corner of Death Valley. If any of you are keen, please meet me by the adventure garage in the parking lot in thirty minutes."

Isla's face lit up. "Can we, Mom? Please? I've never been in a dune buggy!"

Casey saw a flash of concern cross Simone's features, as Maxwell frowned slightly. "Perhaps after you've rested, darling. The flight was—"

"I'll go," Grace interrupted. "I've always wanted to see how these luxury resorts handle their carbon footprint up close."

"It'll be perfect for my channel." Rafael turned to his team. "You stay here, get some B-roll of the place, and I'll take the drone with me."

As Isla continued to plead with her mother, Casey walked over to Simone. "The buggies are very safe, and we'll stay close to the resort for this first tour."

"Oh, let her go," Maxwell said, his attention already shifting to his phone. "Just don't get dirty, angel, and don't touch anything out there."

Arrangements made, the guests dispersed briefly to prepare as Casey slipped out a side door and headed out to ready the buggies for adventure.

CHAPTER 3

CASEY'S BOOTS CRUNCHED ON the sand-dusted concrete of the Sanctuary's garage area.

Desert-adapted equipment filled the staging section: high-end dune buggies in a line out front, their roll cages gleaming in the morning sun. Mountain bikes hung on racks, their specialized tires designed for the harsh terrain. Climbing gear, ropes, carabiners, and harnesses all waited in neat rows.

Casey methodically checked the safety equipment once again, her fingers moving with practiced efficiency over the emergency supplies. Satellite phones, first aid kits, water reserves. Each item carefully maintained and obsessively checked for every trip.

Casey turned at the sound of heavy boots on concrete behind her. Jack walked toward her from the main building, his eyes narrowing at the line of buggies positioned to take guests out on tours.

"These need to be cleared out later," he said without preamble, his voice carrying that edge of assumed command that set Casey's teeth on edge. "Park them somewhere else. I've got a pickup scheduled."

Casey continued her equipment check. "I can probably get it clear by two."

"Make it earlier." Jack took a step closer.

The garage suddenly felt smaller, more confined. Casey forced herself to stand her ground.

She looked up at him, unmoving. "What kind of pickup?"

"Above your pay grade. Just make sure it's clear."

Light footsteps at the garage entrance made Jack step away as Grace Lin entered the structure and stood silhouetted against the desert light. Rafael Ortiz followed close behind, his trademark red bandana already perfectly positioned for maximum camera appeal.

"The social media princess and the wannabe hunter." Jack shook his head and his voice dropped lower, meant for Casey's ears only. "Rather you than me."

High-pitched laughter echoed from the resort. Isla's youthful voice carried on the morning air, full of excitement about the upcoming adventure.

Jack's expression shifted as something dark passed over it. "And the billionaire's brat. What a bunch." He stepped back, already turning away. "Try not to kill anyone out there."

Casey felt a chill down her spine at his words, and her face flushed as he walked away. He must know. Of course, he knew. He would have read her file. Now the bastard would hold it over her.

The morning light shifted as Jack strode toward the exit, his silhouette casting a shadow against the adventure center's back wall. As moved, his shadow merged with another — the sharp spike of a climbing axe that hung from the equipment rack. For a moment, the shadows created the illusion of the metal spike piercing Jack's chest, dark against darker.

Then he walked on and the illusion dissolved as Jack stepped into the full desert sun and seemed to disappear, swallowed by the intensity of the light.

Grace ignored the security chief as she positioned herself for the best angle, taking some selfies with the buggy against the backdrop of the desert.

Rafael turned in place, his phone on a revolving gimbal that would keep the images level, even in a moving vehicle.

"This is going to be epic," he announced to his invisible audience. "Real desert survival, guys. Like our ancestors did it!"

Casey bit back a comment about the difference between surviving in the desert and touring it in a luxury vehicle equipped with satellite phones and emergency supplies.

* * *

Simone tried to catch Isla's hand as they entered the adventure garage. Her daughter practically vibrated with excitement beside her, the girl's energy a stark contrast to Simone's measured steps in her designer sandals.

"Mom, look! They have real climbing gear!" Isla pointed toward the rack of harnesses. "Like the ones in my *National Geographic* magazines!"

Simone squeezed her daughter's hand, savoring these moments when Isla was simply herself, not the carefully groomed heiress Maxwell was determined to shape her into. "Maybe you can do that next time, sweetheart. Let's start with the buggy ride today."

The adventure guide Casey stood by the lead vehicle, checking something under the hood. Her practical clothing and competent movements stirred something in Simone. A memory of freedom, perhaps, from a time before she had chosen the life she lived now.

"Good morning!" Casey straightened from the buggy's engine, wiping her hands on a rag. Her British accent carried clearly in the desert air. "Ready for an adventure?"

Isla ran forward and reached up for the buggy's roll cage. "Can I sit in the front? Please?"

Simone stepped a little closer to Casey. "Will you please take care of her? Keep her safe?"

She caught the flash of something in Casey's eyes. Understanding, perhaps, or recognition of the fear that lurked within every mother's heart.

"Of course." Casey's tone was gentle but confident. "I've got all the safety equipment, plus we won't be gone long. This is just an introductory tour and there's plenty of time during your stay to have another ride."

Simone looked over at Isla, who was now up in the buggy, examining the instruments with fierce concentration. "She needs this. Room to breathe. To explore."

To be something other than Maxwell's perfect daughter.

Casey nodded. "I'm sure she'll enjoy it out there. The desert has a way of showing us who we really are."

Simone gazed out of the garage door, out into the desert, and Casey clearly noticed.

"You could come, too. There's room for one more."

For a moment, Simone imagined what it would be like. The wind in her hair, sun on her skin, speeding away from the hotel onto the salt flats. The open space, the kind of freedom she used to have, before she traded it for Maxwell and his wealth, and what she thought was security.

The thought of him made her catch her breath.

He would hate the thought of his wife bouncing around in a dune buggy like some common tourist. She couldn't risk letting her guard down. At least not for now.

"Thank you, but no." Simone smoothed down her silk dress, an unconscious gesture of submission. "Maybe another time."

Casey's expression softened. "The desert's not going anywhere. It will be out there when you're ready."

Soon, Simone thought, sooner than Casey knew. If everything went to plan.

"I'll leave my daughter in your more than capable hands." Simone turned to Isla, who was fidgeting with impatience up in the buggy. "Be good for Casey, darling. Listen to her instructions."

"I will!" Isla leaned out to plant a quick kiss on her mother's cheek.

The spontaneous gesture made Simone's throat tighten. How much longer would her daughter offer such unguarded affection?

She turned away, leaving Isla to enjoy her adventure, even as she steeled herself for what she must do.

* * *

The dune buggy's engine roared, the sound echoing off the rocky outcrops. Casey eased it into gear, feeling the familiar vibration through the steering wheel as she guided the small group away from the Sanctuary's manicured paths and out into the wilderness beyond.

The morning sun was a molten presence overhead, casting harsh shadows that turned every rock and scrub bush into potential shelter for the desert's more lethal residents.

In her side mirror, Casey watched Grace Lin arrange herself in the back seat as if posing for a magazine shoot. The influencer's perfectly manicured hands kept rising to smooth her hair, fighting a losing battle against the hot wind that whipped through the open-air vehicle. Her phone was already out, angled for maximum effect against the backdrop of the Amargosa Range.

"Wait, wait. Stop here. The light's fantastic," Grace called out in the particular tone of someone used to being obeyed. "I want to catch the mountains behind me."

Casey pretended not to hear and pressed the accelerator instead.

They were far too close to the resort to get any good footage. Grace would forget her annoyance soon enough once she saw what was ahead.

Rafael sat with a rifle across his lap. His hands moved over the weapon, adjusting his grip, impatient for violence.

"See that ridgeline?" He pointed. "Bet there's bighorn sheep up there. You ready to watch some authentic survival skills?"

"You mean watch you murder for clicks?" Grace's voice dripped with disdain. "Those sheep are protected, anyway."

"Protected?" Rafael laughed. "By who? City people who've never had to hunt their own food? This is nature. Kill or be killed."

Casey's fingers tightened on the wheel. The desert was lethal enough without adding human predators to the mix.

She had researched Death Valley's flora and fauna extensively before taking this job, learning habits and patterns, and strategies for survival in this harshest of environments. Each creature and plant played its role in a delicate balance that had evolved over millennia, and this man would destroy it in an instant for entertainment. She bit back all the words she wanted to say.

"Look! What's that?" Isla shouted, twisting in her seat, pointing at a flash of movement among the creosote bushes.

Casey slowed the buggy and let the engine idle. "I think it was a desert kit fox," she explained, grateful for the distraction. "Did you see how small it was? Those huge ears help them stay cool and hear prey underground."

"It was so cute!" Isla bounced in her seat, her energy seemingly unaffected by the growing heat. "What else lives out here? Are there snakes? What about those big crow things I saw earlier?"

"Those were ravens," Casey said, easing the buggy on. "They're incredibly intelligent. The local Timbisha Shoshone people believe they're messengers between our world and the spirit world."

She glanced at Rafael, who was now sighting with his rifle into the bushes, clearly hoping for a glimpse of the fox. "They're also protected by law, like all creatures here."

Rafael lowered his weapon with a snort. "Everything's protected these days. But out here? Who's going to know?"

"I'll know," Casey said quietly, her words lost in the wind.

She spotted a patch of yellow flowers, a chance to change the focus of the tour. "Look there. See that patch of desert marigolds? They only bloom after the rain, so we're lucky to see them."

Isla grinned. "They're so pretty!"

"Let me show you somewhere even prettier." Casey steered the buggy toward Artists Palette and soon the multi-colored rocks loomed ahead, their bands of color stark against the pale sky in shades of rust, dusky pink, acid green, and royal purple.

"The colors come from different minerals in the rock," Casey explained. "The red and pink are from iron, the purple from manganese, and the green is from decomposed, tuff-derived mica."

The words were familiar, grounding the tour in repetition.

"Nature is the greatest artist," Grace said, her voice softer now she was happy catching the beauty of the landscape on her phone. "This light is incredible. The way it catches the minerals."

Casey nodded. "The colors change throughout the day as the sun moves. They're most vibrant at sunset. I'll park up ahead and you can all explore a little."

As they rounded a bend, a dark opening appeared in the rock face up on the cliffs to their left.

"Are there caves?" Isla asked excitedly, pointing at the shadowy void. "Can we go in them?"

"No!" The word burst from Casey's lips like a gunshot.

Too sharp. Too loud.

CHAPTER 4

Isla flinched, hurt flickering across her face, and for Casey, the desert heat suddenly felt very far away.

She was back in the Mendips, deep in the cave system. Damp air filled her lungs as the beam of her headlamp caught Eric's terrified face below her.

He was one of her school students on a weeks' caving expedition and when he had gotten stuck in a vertical shaft, Casey had at first tried to keep the situation light. It was a chance to educate them on what to do when things didn't go according to plan.

But their laughter soon died away, replaced by the sound of Eric's increasingly panicked breathing echoing off the limestone walls.

"Just stay calm, Eric. It's going to be fine."

But it wasn't fine.

A narrow dogleg shaft had trapped him in an angled section. Each movement only wedged him tighter, each panicked breath using up more of the precious oxygen in that confined space.

Casey sent the other teacher and the rest of the students on up to the surface to get them to safety and call the rescue team. As the leader, she stayed with Eric, telling him stories of all the times she'd explored down here. There had been difficulties, and they had always made it out.

But she'd watched helplessly as his struggles grew weaker, as his breath rasped and the light in his eyes dimmed.

Casey tried to wind back time. She shouldn't have taken them this way. She shouldn't have tried the dogleg tunnel. She should have avoided the vertical shaft.

When the rescue team finally reached them, they found Casey sitting on the edge of the shaft, weeping. They said Eric had likely gone quickly, suffocated by the carbon dioxide in the vertical tube-like tunnel. He wouldn't have suffered long.

But Casey knew better.

She had witnessed his final gasping breaths, seen the terror in his eyes as he realized no one could reach him in time.

His parents made the decision to seal the shaft with his body still inside. A rock and concrete tomb, marked with a small bronze plaque where their son lay forever in darkness.

The resulting investigation had cleared her.

Casey had followed every safety protocol, checked every piece of equipment before descending. She had followed the exploration plan filed with the authorities. But that didn't stop the whispers in the small Somerset village, the sidelong glances from parents who'd trusted her with their children. It didn't stop her partner from leaving, unable to handle her descent into guilt-ridden depression.

So she had fled, as far as she could, from the damp, close caves of the Mendip Hills.

Here in Death Valley, everything was surface and sky. The landscape was stripped bare, honest in its dangers. Nothing hidden.

But she would not go back into any kind of cave, and she would not adventure below ground.

Casey forced herself back into the present, to the hot desert air and the concerned expressions at her tone.

"I'm sorry, Isla. I didn't mean to snap. But look —" She pointed at a carpark ahead overlooking the most stunning section of Artists Palette. "We don't need to go in the caves. Look what we can see over there."

Casey gestured at the vast expanse of low rocky hills before them. "The alluvial fans spread out from the canyons. Each one tells a story of flash floods and debris flow, of rocks ground to sand over millions of years."

Isla's curiosity returned. "What's an alluvial fan?"

Casey latched onto the question, grateful for the distraction.

As she explained the geology, she kept her eyes fixed firmly on the horizon, where heat waves shimmered above the salt pans, pushing away the memories, the weight of the earth above her, the dank cave air at the back of her throat.

A minute later, Casey pulled in and parked the buggy on the ridge overlooking Artists Palette, turning off the engine.

For a moment, the abrupt silence amplified the vastness of the vista before them as endless waves of rock and sand stretched to the horizon. The mineral-stained cliffs blazed with color in the sunlight, their bands of rusty red and poisonous green seeming to pulse in the rising heat.

The group clambered out, and both Grace and Rafael headed for the lookout.

"Stay back from the edge," Casey warned. "The rock can be unstable, and it's a long way down."

She'd seen the statistics and read the accident reports. Tourists who thought they were invincible, who forgot the desert's lethal indifference to human life. A surprising number plummeted to their deaths while taking selfies.

Isla bounced from rock to rock, her earlier hurt forgotten in the excitement of exploration. "Look how high we are! You can see everything!"

Casey tracked the girl's movement. Too many loose rocks, too many hidden cracks that could twist an ankle. Or worse. Time for a distraction.

"Isla, come and see this."

Casey patted the smooth rock beside her, well back from the edge. "Let me show you something interesting while the others take their photos."

Isla bounded over, but up close, Casey noticed a shadow behind the girl's enthusiasm, a certain watchfulness in her eyes that seemed too old for her eleven years.

"See these marks in the stone?" Casey traced her finger along the faint parallel grooves. "Water made these. Millions of years ago, sharks swam right where we're sitting."

Isla's eyes widened. "Really? Sharks in the desert?"

"It wasn't a desert then. Everything was underwater, but it still holds all kinds of secrets."

Casey reached into her pack and pulled out her water bottle. "Speaking of secrets, want to learn one about surviving out here?"

The girl nodded eagerly, settling closer.

"Here." Casey handed her the bottle. "Take a small sip, but don't swallow. Just hold it in your mouth for a moment."

Isla followed the instruction, her expression curious.

"Feel how it cools you down? That's a trick I learned from the local Timbisha people. In the desert, you have to make every drop count."

Casey demonstrated, taking her own small sip. "Too many tourists come out here and chug their water. They end up dehydrated twice as fast."

"Like Dad with his protein shakes," Isla muttered, then looked away quickly, as if she'd said too much.

Casey kept her voice casual. "Does your dad drink a lot of those?"

"All the time. And these gross smoothies that smell weird." Isla wrinkled her nose and pulled her knees to her chest. "He has all these charts and graphs about optimizing his nutrition. He got mad at Mom last week because the cook made pasta for dinner. He said it wasn't 'aligned with his new program.' But I love pasta."

Casey had read about Maxwell's health obsession in the guest briefing documents, but she hadn't considered how that fixation might affect his daughter.

"Sometimes grownups get too focused on things," Casey said carefully. "Especially things they're afraid of losing."

"He's afraid of getting old." Isla picked up a small stone and turned it over in her hands. "I heard him yelling at Mom. He said she wasn't trying hard enough to stay young. That she was letting herself go." She threw the stone with sudden force and it skittered across the rocks toward the edge. "I hate when he shouts."

Casey watched the stone disappear into the vastness below. "You know it's not your fault that he shouts, right?"

"I guess." Isla traced the water-carved grooves on the rock with gentle fingers. "Mom cries sometimes when she thinks I can't hear. And she keeps checking her face in mirrors, looking for wrinkles. I wish…" she trailed off, blinking hard.

"What do you wish?"

"I wish they could just be normal, like my friend Ella's parents. Her dad takes us hiking sometimes and her mom lets us pack sandwiches with white bread, and we look for lizards together."

A tear slipped down her cheek. "I don't like Ella to come to my house. It's not fun. Everything has to be perfect. The right clothes, the right food, the right everything. Like a museum where you can't touch anything."

Casey's chest tightened. She recognized that feeling. The weight of other people's expectations, the pressure to maintain an image that slowly suffocated the real person beneath.

She'd felt it after Eric's death, when her whole community seemed to watch, judging, waiting for her to either break down or prove herself worthy of forgiveness. She hoped that somehow Isla would find her way out. Perhaps this week Casey could help her a little.

"Want to learn another desert secret?" she asked, reaching into her pack again.

Isla nodded, wiping her eyes quickly.

Casey pulled out a small magnifying glass. "Look at this." She held it over a patch of seemingly bare rock. "What do you see?"

Isla peered through the lens, then gasped. "Tiny plants! They're growing right out of the stone!"

"Desert flowers," Casey confirmed. "Most people walk right past them, thinking nothing could survive here. But life finds a way, even in the hardest places. These little plants don't care about being perfect. They just keep growing, keep adapting, keep being exactly what they are. Sometimes, after the floods, the whole desert blooms."

Isla studied the miniature ecosystem for a long moment, then looked up at Casey with a hint of her natural brightness returning. "Can we find more?"

"Of course." Casey smiled. She looked over to check that Grace and Rafael were still occupied with their respective photo shoots.

Grace had found a perfect spot, artfully arranging herself before the backdrop of the painted cliffs.

Her phone was mounted on a collapsible tripod, and she moved through a series of practiced poses with professional precision. "The light is absolutely perfect," she murmured, checking her screen. "My followers are going to love this. #DeathValleyDreams #WildernessLuxury."

Casey noticed Grace was inching backwards with each shot, getting closer to the edge in search of the perfect angle.

"That's far enough, Ms. Lin," she called out, keeping her voice casual but firm.

Rafael wandered off to the side, his rifle at the ready as he shuffled to the edge. His weapon looked wrong here, an intrusion of manufactured death in a landscape that handled its killing with far more elegance.

Casey divided her attention between him and the others, hyper-aware of the various ways this situation could go wrong as she pointed out lizard tracks for Isla to follow.

The sudden crack of the rifle split the air.

Ravens wheeled up from the rocks as the sound echoed around the cliffs.

Casey's hand went instinctively to her radio, but what would she report? Tara had cleared Rafael's hunting, so everything was legal on paper, even if it felt like sacrilege.

Rafael emerged from behind a boulder, triumphantly holding a limp desert cottontail rabbit by its legs. The animal's soft fur was matted with blood, its eyes already glazing over.

"A little snack to get us started," he announced, playing to his invisible audience, captured by the camera drone circling around him. "This is real food, amigos. No supermarket, no fancy packaging. Just man versus nature."

He pulled out a hunting knife, the blade catching the sun like a mirror, and began to skin the rabbit on top of a rock, his movements quick and practiced.

The wet sound of the blade separating flesh from fur caused Grace to cry out. "You monster! That rabbit was a living creature, not a prop for your blood sport entertainment!"

"Circle of life, princess." Rafael didn't even look up. "Humans are predators. Some of us haven't forgotten that."

His hands moved efficiently, stripping away the rabbit's soft pelt to expose the pink skin beneath. "Besides, your daddy's companies have destroyed more lives than I ever could in several lifetimes."

Grace flinched, and something more complicated than anger flashed across her face.

Isla edged closer to Rafael's impromptu butcher station, her eyes wide with fascination.

"Is that really what it looks like inside?" She pointed to the exposed organs. "We only see pictures in science class."

Rafael grinned, clearly happy to have an appreciative audience. "Want to feel the heart? It's still warm."

"Isla, I don't think—" Casey started, but the girl had already reached out.

Her small fingers touched the rabbit's heart gently, leaving a smear of blood on her skin.

"It's so soft," Isla whispered, a mix of horror and wonder in her voice. "And tiny."

Blood dripped onto the pale rock, stark red against the mineral-stained surface. Some primal part of Casey's brain recognized the scene. Life and death played out against an ancient backdrop, as it had been for millions of years.

But the rest of her saw only the spreading stains on Isla's clothes and imagined trying to explain this to Simone.

Grace had turned away, but her phone was still recording. Probably planning to edit this into some kind of environmental statement piece.

Rafael continued his work, now arranging the rabbit's organs in a neat display, naming each one for Isla's education.

The girl's initial squeamishness had given way to genuine curiosity, and she peppered him with questions about anatomy and hunting techniques.

Casey watched them, feeling the weight of responsibility press down like the desert heat. A responsible luxury adventure guide would surely stop this impromptu biology lesson and protect Isla's innocence. But wasn't this more honest than the sanitized version of nature most American children saw?

The desert was brutal. Life and death, predator and prey, survival written in blood on stone.

Above them, against the gathering clouds, two ravens circled back, waiting for their share of the kill.

CHAPTER 5

Simone was still thinking of Isla as she hurried back to the Sanctuary's premier private villa. The porters arriving with their extensive luggage soon consumed her attention and she directed them with a choreographed skill honed by years of traveling in luxury.

The suite angled before her in shades of sand and stone. Reclaimed wooden shades artfully directed beams of light, keeping the full strength of the sun out while still making the high-ceilinged rooms feel spacious and bright. Pale limestone tiles stood out against walls textured to mimic wind-carved canyon walls, with accents of burnished copper gleaming like the desert at sunset.

An elegant piece of local art dominated one wall. A topographical map rendered in layers of glass and metal with silhouettes of circling ravens worked into the piece, their wings forever frozen mid-flight against a bright sky.

Simone pushed aside her nervous preoccupation to enjoy the understated taste of the suite's furnishings. The designers had brought the best of the desert inside while keeping its dangers at bay. The mesquite wood furniture echoed the organic curves of sand dunes, upholstered in fabrics dyed with local tones of deep rust and pale gold. Hand-woven rugs traced patterns like dry riverbeds across the floor, their muted colors a perfect match for the desert palette beyond the high windows.

Simone glanced out to see the Amargosa Range stretching to the horizon. The mountains seemed to ripple in the heat haze, making them appear both impossibly close and eternally unreachable. She found herself drawn by the vast emptiness beyond, and the suite's artificial cool fell away as Simone imagined herself out there, away from the suffocating weight of perfection that pressed down on her every day, away from—

"Where shall I put this, ma'am?"

A porter cleared his throat politely behind her, pulling her back to the present moment. He pushed a small medical-grade refrigeration unit that was now an essential part of every trip.

Simone pointed to an alcove near the master bedroom. "Over there will be fine. Careful with it, please."

The young porter nodded, struggling slightly with the sleek unit.

Simone watched him, remembering how she had carried drink trays with the same careful attention, back when she'd been an aspiring actress in LA, working as a cocktail waitress on the side and dreaming of escape. Now she wore Louboutins that cost more than her annual rent back then. But despite the luxury surrounding her, that sense of smothered dreams, that longing for the horizon she'd felt in her waitressing days had come creeping back.

The porter carefully positioned the refrigeration unit and plugged it in, the soft mechanical drone a reminder of its precious cargo.

Simone checked the temperature display, her manicured fingers hovering over the controls. "Perfect, thank you."

The porter hovered by the door, eager to earn his tip. "Is there anything else you need, Mrs. Carver-Scott?"

"No, thank you. That's everything for now." She pulled a

hundred-dollar bill from her Hermès wallet and handed it to him.

The young porter's eyes widened slightly as he accepted it. Good. Let word spread through the staff that she was generous and kind.

It might matter later.

Through the patio doors, she heard the splash of Maxwell entering the villa's infinity pool.

Simone walked over to watch him power through a lap and tumble turn at the end. The water sparkled as he cut through it with practiced strokes; beyond the pool's edge, the desert stretched vast and empty. The contrast was stark. An oasis of luxury floating above a merciless landscape, and with every second, more of this water evaporated.

Maxwell saw her and called out between laps. "Darling, join me?"

"Later, perhaps." She touched her perfectly styled hair. "I should unpack."

He grunted and resumed swimming, already focused entirely on his workout.

Despite his sixty-two years, Maxwell's disciplined exercise regime kept his body firm and strong. Simone watched him count his laps under his breath, the same number he'd done since his college swimming days, as if hitting that metric daily could somehow hold back time.

She pushed the patio door closed to keep the heat out and walked through to the master bathroom, her slim figure reflected in multiple mirrors along the way.

Her dress skimmed over slight curves maintained by brutal workouts and long days of intermittent fasting, the pale coral silk making her honey-colored skin glow.

Dark hair fell in expensive layers around her face. It was not quite black, but the rich brown of bitter chocolate, artfully streaked with caramel highlights that caught the light as she moved. Simone was well aware of her looks. She had the kind of beauty that turned heads but didn't overwhelm, and her delicate features were arranged with perfect symmetry. She was both striking and somehow approachable. Her beauty had served her well as an aspiring actress — and even better as a trophy wife.

Simone checked the placement of their toiletries, rearranging Maxwell's razor so it lay at the precise angle he preferred. Every detail mattered in their choreographed life. One misstep could fracture the perfect illusion she'd worked so hard to maintain, and on this trip, everything needed to remain the same — at least, until she was ready to make the change.

She studied her reflection in the gilded mirror, adopting the pose she knew best flattered her angles.

At forty-five, she still retained the natural beauty that Maxwell had first seen in her. The extensive skincare regime and carefully scheduled procedures saw to that.

But she could see what Maxwell increasingly saw. The first hints of crow's feet, the slight softening along her jaw, the whispered suggestion of mortality that no amount of Botox could completely erase.

She was still beautiful, yes, but her beauty required more maintenance with each passing year, like one of Maxwell's vintage sports cars that needed increasingly expensive parts to keep running.

Her body betrayed her in new ways too, ways she couldn't always hide behind designer clothes and careful makeup. The night sweats that woke her, forcing her to change into a fresh nightdress so Maxwell wouldn't notice. The mood swings that came out of nowhere with rage and despair washing over her in waves she couldn't control. The unfamiliar fluctuations in her body temperature — one moment freezing in the air conditioning, the next burning up despite it.

She had researched everything she could about

perimenopause, but kept her browser history carefully cleared. Maxwell couldn't know. While he kept his vintage cars lovingly maintained in climate-controlled garages, he did not keep his wives.

Simone dabbed at a bead of sweat on her upper lip, remembering the look on his second wife's face when Maxwell had first brought Simone to a charity gala just over fifteen years ago.

Patricia had known exactly what it meant, the same way that Simone now recognized the signs with Maxwell's gorgeous executive assistant, Emma. The late nights at the office, the private jet trips, the way Maxwell's hand lingered on Emma's arm during meetings.

Simone had been the other woman once, as Patricia aged out of Maxwell's acceptable range. She had been so certain it would be different for her, that youth and beauty would somehow never slip from her grasp. But the years ticked by, regardless.

Simone's hand shook slightly as she reapplied her lipstick.

She had made her choice back then, giving up her nascent acting career for a man decades older than her. She raised his child and organized his life and subjugated her ambition — and her youth — to his needs.

She transformed into the perfect corporate wife, learned about wine and art, and mastered the social dynamics of Silicon Valley's elite. She thought all those efforts would secure her future, but they meant nothing when weighed against the wrinkles on her skin.

Back then, Simone had signed an extensive prenuptial agreement. The optimism of youth made the terms seem generous, especially as she never expected it to be used. She would be provided for, and any children protected.

But she hadn't read the fine print carefully enough, and when she noticed Maxwell's gaze falling on Emma, Simone had dug the document out of her personal papers.

If Maxwell divorced her, Isla would still be wealthy, like all his children, but once her daughter turned eighteen, Simone's alimony payments would drop sharply. She'd have enough to keep up appearances, but certainly not enough to maintain the lifestyle she'd sacrificed everything for.

But if Maxwell died…

Simone took a deep breath and opened her designer makeup bag, methodically checking each product. The familiar ritual usually calmed her, but today her hands trembled.

Seeing Jack complicated things.

She had planned this trip carefully, each detail orchestrated toward a specific outcome. But Jack was a wild card.

He recognized her, that was for sure, and his presence here made Simone consider whether she needed to wait to put her plan into action. He had aged well in the fifteen years since they'd last been together, his military bearing giving him a timeless masculine quality that all of Maxwell's fastidious maintenance could never match.

Simone traced a finger along the cool marble of the bathroom counter, remembering those stolen moments with Jack between her auditions and his security shifts.

He was assigned as security after she landed a minor role in an action movie filming in Mexico, her one legitimate break before reality forced her back to cocktail waitressing. Their professional relationship quickly evolved into something more primal. Simone closed her eyes, sensing the desert heat seeping through the windows despite the air conditioning.

She could almost feel Jack's rough hands on her skin, the way he pushed her up against a wall, taking her to the edge of pleasure, their every touch raw with need for each other.

The splash of the pool outside brought her back to the present.

Simone calmed her breathing. She didn't have much time left to decide.

Maxwell measured his strokes, each lap identical to the last, counting down until he completed his target. On time, every time.

Everything about him was controlled and optimized. Even their sex life was an item on his schedule, tracked and analyzed like his workout routine.

Jack had been nothing like that.

Sure, he talked about survival and tactical advantage while trailing kisses down her neck, but his obsessions somehow made him more alive, more present in the moment. He would lose himself in her and all would be forgotten, at least for a time.

Perhaps she could have been happy with Jack if she had been content with simple pleasures, but he was too unpredictable, and too focused on preparing for some imagined apocalypse, to offer the lifestyle she wanted and the wealth she craved.

When Maxwell had shown interest in her as she waitressed at a business conference, Simone seized her chance. She leveraged her beauty and youth, transforming from waitress to executive assistant to lover with a tactical precision Jack might have appreciated — if she hadn't left him behind without even a goodbye.

Now Jack was here, and he had always been able to read her, to see past her carefully constructed facade. He had known her back in her acting days, and this trip required her to perform the most challenging role she'd ever attempted.

Maxwell's counting grew louder outside as he pushed himself through his final laps.

Seventy-eight, seventy-nine, eighty.

Each number precise and measured, like everything else in his life. Soon, he would want his treatment. He always did after swimming. Something about exercise optimizing absorption.

Simone glanced at her diamond Cartier watch, calculating the timing. Everything had to be perfect.

She walked back through the suite and bent to the refrigeration unit, opening it carefully. The soft click of the seal breaking barely registered over the drone of the pool filter.

The bags of blood lay nestled in their temperature-controlled chamber, each one labeled with alpha-numeric codes that revealed nothing about their young athletic male donors. Clean, clinical, anonymous bags of possibility purchased at astronomical prices.

Simone's hand trembled slightly as she reached into the back of the refrigeration unit.

There. The bag she'd prepared back in LA, its code matching the others perfectly.

She eased it forward, positioning it precisely where she would reach for the next batch. The liquid inside was darker than the others, but only slightly. Not enough to notice unless you were looking for it, and Maxwell never prepared his own IV. That was one of her jobs.

She closed the door softly and stood up, smoothing her sundress with hands that felt suddenly cold despite the desert heat seeping through the windows.

For a moment, she simply stood there, listening to the splash of the pool, the hum of air conditioning, the sound of her own heart beating in her ears. She could empty the bag out right now, flush the evidence away. Maxwell would be none the wiser.

Emma's knowing smile flashed through Simone's memory. Had the girl even looked at her with a hint of pity when she'd seen them off at the airport?

Simone took a deep breath, walked to the closet, and pulled out her new La Perla bikini. The fabric was the exact shade of pale coral that Maxwell once said brought out the honey tones in her skin.

She hesitated only a moment before changing. Everything had to appear normal. Perfect. Expected.

CHAPTER 6

MAXWELL COUNTED EACH STROKE with practiced precision as his arms cut through the water in perfect arcs.

Seventy-eight. Seventy-nine. Eighty.

The rhythm was embedded in his muscle memory, unchanged since his days as Stanford swim captain in '83. His reflection rippled across the infinity edge of the pool, fragmenting against the stark backdrop of Death Valley's desert landscape that stretched endlessly below.

He glimpsed the desert's harsh beauty sprawled beyond the pool's edge as he swam. It was indifferent to his internal battles. The wind-carved rocks were evidence of millions of years of entropy, but Maxwell refused to accept the same inevitability for his own flesh.

Another tumble-turn.

The familiar push off the wall sent water streaming past his ears. He could still execute the movement with the same tight efficiency he'd mastered over fifty years ago, though it required more effort now.

Everything required more effort now.

His sleek sports watch vibrated against his wrist. Heart rate 132, slightly elevated for this stage of his workout. He adjusted his stroke rate, moderating his pace.

The watch was just one node in the network of biomarkers

he monitored constantly. Sleep cycles, glucose levels, tes-tosterone, inflammatory markers, and so many more. The data streamed to servers where algorithms analyzed every variant, seeking patterns that indicated a whisper of decay and suggesting the optimum regime to offset it.

Through the rippling water, he saw Simone emerge onto the pool deck. Even distorted by the liquid lens, he could read the subtle signs of age beginning to etch themselves into her form.

The slight softening along her jaw. The way gravity pulled at the flesh of her upper arms and breasts despite her rigor-ous workouts and the procedures he insisted upon.

She was still beautiful — his wealth and her discipline ensured that — but she was a reminder of everything he fought against.

He broke the surface, taking another stroke as Simone arranged herself on one of the custom loungers, her bikini exactly matching the coral highlights in the hand-laid pool tiles.

She was always perfectly coordinated, always camera-ready. He had been attracted to that precision when he'd first noticed her. The way she anticipated his needs before he voiced them, the elegant efficiency of her movements. But she'd been in her late twenties then, radiant with the unconscious vitality of youth.

A vitality he now found in Emma, his newly promoted head of special projects. She was less than half his age, but her ambition burned as bright as his own and her energy was still untamed. She understood his vision for the future, not just for his companies, but for humanity itself.

All that drive spilled over into their frenzied lovemaking, and the age difference meant nothing when their energy matched one another's.

Maxwell pushed off for another lap.

The young blood treatments were clearly working. He

could feel it in the resilience of his muscles, in the clarity of his thoughts. His stamina matching Emma's.

The entrepreneur and bio-hacker Bryan Johnson had shared data showing cognitive improvements of twenty percent after six months of parabiosis: the introduction of young blood into the old. Maxwell's own numbers tracked similarly, and he longed for even more improvement.

As Maxwell tumble-turned again, he remembered the words of his first swim coach. "Your body is a machine. Maintain it properly and it will serve you forever." Machines could be upgraded, optimized, and their parts replaced. Why should organic matter be any different?

He glanced over at Simone between strokes.

He had shown her research papers, the brain scans, the telomere studies, all evidence that young blood — taken from highly screened and willing participants, of course — could wind back the clock.

But she recoiled in disgust. He'd tuned out the specifics of her objections; some antiquated ethical framework prevented her from embracing the possibilities, he gathered. Disappointing, but perhaps unsurprising. She was never his equal when it came to a vision of the future. Not like Emma.

A dark shape caught Maxwell's eye just meters away at the end of the pool.

A scorpion emerged from the carefully curated desert garden that bordered the deck. Its segmented tail curled overhead, its stinger poised as it scuttled across the tiles. A reminder that death was always close out here in the desert.

A cloud passed overhead, casting the deck into momentary shadow. The scorpion scuttled away.

Maxwell hoisted himself out of the pool, water dripping off muscles maintained by daily workouts and carefully calibrated hormone optimization. Sixty-two years old, and he could still complete the same number of laps he had done at twenty.

But it wasn't enough.

There was too much to accomplish, too many frontiers to cross. The latest rumors from his Silicon Valley network hinted at neural mapping breakthroughs and the possibility of uploading consciousness itself.

But that technology was still theoretical and the timeline uncertain. For now, he needed his organic machine operating at peak efficiency.

"I'm heading in," he told Simone.

She nodded without looking up from her phone, another reminder of their growing disconnection.

Perhaps he should wait to tell her about the divorce until they returned home after this holiday. Let her enjoy these last days of luxury. He'd be generous with the settlement. He always was. It was good business practice, and he prided himself on approaching every aspect of life with strategic precision.

Maxwell grabbed a heated towel from the warming drawer in the bathroom and dried himself quickly. The day's schedule stretched ahead. His IV treatment, then calls with his quantum computing team, then some ridiculous banquet dinner where he'd have to maintain the fiction of being a happy family for Isla's sake.

Time ticked relentlessly on, but he would fight it every day and claw back his youth, no matter the cost.

He checked the app on his phone that synced with his watch, swiping through the biometric data with satisfaction at the results. His heart rate during the swim had maintained optimal zones, his oxygen saturation remained perfect, his hormone levels stayed within carefully calibrated ranges.

He swiped to a different screen.

"Simone." He kept his voice neutral, controlled, even as irritation prickled under his skin. "Come here a minute."

She walked in from the deck.

Once, that coral bikini would have made his pulse

quicken, but now he only noticed how the fabric stretched slightly at the seams and how her skin had lost some of its elasticity.

"What is it?" Her tone was perfect, her practiced concern masking wariness. She'd gotten better at that over the years, learning to modulate her responses just as he modulated his biochemistry.

"Your cortisol levels are elevated." He pulled up the graph on his phone, expanding it to fill the screen. "And your estrogen is fluctuating wildly. Look at these patterns over the last few weeks."

She stiffened. "You're monitoring my hormones?"

"Of course." He zoomed in on a particularly concerning spike. "The sensors I had installed in our bathroom mirror track basic biometrics. Your skin elasticity has decreased 3.2 percent in the last month alone. And these stress markers…" He shook his head. "The data suggests you're entering peri-menopause."

He almost spat the last word, barely suppressing a shudder at the thought of her age-racked body if she continued to let the situation slide.

Simone's carefully maintained composure cracked, just for a moment. He caught a flash of rage in her eyes before she smoothed it away. Another imperfection, another sign of hormonal imbalance.

"I'm forty-five, Maxwell. It's natural—"

"Natural?" He cut her off. "Cancer is natural. Death is natural. The whole point is to transcend nature."

He set the phone down. "I've already spoken to Dr. Matsuda. He can start you on the young blood treatments immediately. If you combine it with extended hormone optimization—"

"No." The word was flat, final.

"Don't be irrational. My biological age has actually reversed by—"

"I said no." Simone's voice carried an edge he hadn't heard before. "I won't be one of your experiments."

"Experiments?" His fists clenched. "I'm trying to help you. To save you from—"

"From what? From being human?" She gestured at the array of medical equipment that filled one corner of their suite. "Look at yourself, Maxwell. All these treatments, all these measurements. You're so afraid of death you've forgotten how to live."

Maxwell forced himself to breathe evenly, to maintain homeostasis despite the surge of adrenaline her defiance triggered.

"This is about evolution." His voice remained steady through sheer force of will. "About transcending biological limitation. The young blood treatments are just the beginning. With the novel forms of AI-driven scientific discovery, we're on the verge of immortality."

"And what about Isla?" Simone said softly. "While you obsess over your precious data, your daughter is growing up. Do you even notice? Or is she just another metric to optimize?"

Maxwell picked up his phone again and pulled up another screen. Isla's growth charts, her cognitive assessments, her genetic potential mapped out in clean lines and color-coded projections.

"Of course I notice. I track everything. Her development is precisely—"

"That's not what I mean and you know it." Simone stepped closer.

He caught the scent of her skin. Another imperfection, as the expensive perfume failed to mask her natural chemistry, which had changed with her shifting hormones.

"When was the last time you played with her?" Simone demanded. "Or read her a story? Or asked her about her day at school without turning it into a data point?"

"Sentiment clouds clear judgment." Maxwell turned away, unable to look anymore at the signs of aging around her eyes. "I'm trying to create a future where she'll never have to watch her father grow old and die. Where she can—"

"What? Upload her consciousness? Turn herself into pure data without the burden of flesh? She needs a father, Maxwell. Not a trans-human experiment."

She took a deep breath and sighed, reached out a hand to him, then dropped it to one side. "You must do as you see fit, and of course, I will help you achieve your health goals. But please, enough about me and Isla. Let me enjoy the pool while you shower."

Simone turned and walked back out onto the deck, reclining as she stared out at the desert beyond. Maxwell watched her for a moment through the window, cataloging each of her flaws and her every deviation from the ideal.

She once understood his vision and shared his drive for perfection. Or perhaps that had all been part of her performance, another role played by a struggling actress to get close to him? Well, she better make the most of it while she still had access to all this luxury.

Maxwell turned away from the view of his wife, his mind turning to the lithe, youthful figure of Emma, smiling as he headed into the shower. The future was bright indeed.

CHAPTER 7

JACK SCANNED THE BANK of security monitors, each screen a window into the carefully maintained illusion of the Sanctuary.

The security room hummed with the sound of fans and surveillance equipment, the temperature kept even cooler than the rest of the hotel to protect the electronics. But even here, the desert air seeped in somehow, carrying the mineral scent of sunbaked stone and creosote.

Jack adjusted the angle of a camera tracking movement by the pool area of the most luxurious villa.

Simone Carver-Scott came into sharp focus.

Fifteen years hadn't dimmed her beauty or her calculated grace as she arranged herself on a lounger, and the sight of her triggered memories he thought he'd buried long ago. Her soft laughter as they took their pleasure together between security shifts, the way she'd played at being the struggling actress for him while clearly hunting bigger prey.

He was young and naïve back then, fresh out of the military and wide-eyed at the chance of a Hollywood fairy tale. But now he recognized her type. She was a survivor, yes, but one who relied on others rather than her own capabilities.

Jack felt a flicker of pity and quickly suppressed it. The weak and dependent would not survive the conflict that was inevitably coming to this broken, hollowed-out country where divisions deepened every day. That was the law of nature, as old as the desert itself.

The tactical watch on his wrist vibrated. Another hour gone.

Jack logged the time into his schedule and reviewed his checklist of threats and risks.

Desert creatures were one of the many hazards and usually his various safeguards kept most of them out. On this occasion, they were already inside. Not for long though, since he expected to get these shipped out within a few hours, and the money would be in his account by tomorrow.

He touched the screen, shifting to a view of the interior desert garden, adjusting the angle to check on his investment.

The six desert horned vipers lay coiled in their secure terrarium, barely visible among the rocks and plants. Their venom sacs were full, and each would fetch top dollar from his contact in the underground medicinal trade.

The snakes represented another step toward Jack's true goal, a compound he was building in the Ozarks, far from the civilizational collapse he and many others in the prepper community knew was coming.

"Time's running out," he murmured as he pulled up the satellite weather feed on another monitor.

A storm system was building much faster than predicted, with bands of pressure and temperature that might sweep down the valley over the hotel if the wind changed direction.

He didn't need to act right now, as so often these systems dissipated before they reached the Sanctuary, but it was something to keep an eye on.

The radio at his hip crackled. "Security, this is maintenance. AC unit three is showing fluctuations again."

"Copy that." Jack's response was automatic as he logged the issue.

Just another crack in the Sanctuary's facade, which, like everything man-made, fought against nature daily in a struggle to resist entropy and collapse.

His deployment in Afghanistan had taught him how quickly infrastructure could fail, and how thin the line between order and chaos really was. The Sanctuary's guests, cushioned by wealth and privilege, would never see the signs before disaster hit, but Jack could see the patterns everywhere in modern day America. Supply chain disruption, social unrest, the slow erosion of systems people took for granted. It was all spiraling to an inglorious end, just like every other empire that died when its people became too fat and weak and entitled.

But some would survive, and he intended to be one of those who would rise from the ashes of a doomed nation to build anew.

The snake venom was just one in a string of similar ventures. All of them, like armed shipment escorts and private security contracts, blurred the boundaries of legal and illegal activities. And each job put more dollars into his bug-out fund, strengthening Jack's position for when everything finally broke down.

Some called him paranoid. He called it prepared.

A movement on the premium villa monitor caught his attention.

Maxwell Carver-Scott strolled back out onto the pool deck and said something to Simone as he stared out at the desert before him.

Jack's lip curled. All that wealth, all that power, and Maxwell was still just prey, desperately trying to outrun his own mortality.

The desert beyond the pool shimmered with lethal heat, its vast emptiness calling to something primitive in Jack's blood. This artificial oasis couldn't last. Nothing built by human hands could stand against nature's patience.

The thought brought a grim smile to his face. Let the guests play at their sanitized wilderness adventures. He knew what real survival looked like.

He checked the terrarium again. The snakes would be gone soon, handed off to his contact during the next supply delivery, and if that bitch Casey cleared out the garage area in time as he asked, it could be done under cover in the cool. A clean transaction, just like the others.

Jack pulled up his project tracking app, checking the numbers that marched upward and to the right in neat columns. Precious metals, cryptocurrency, ammunition stockpiles. Each category another layer of security against the coming chaos. The total was impressive, but still shy of what he needed for complete self-sufficiency over the years the conflict was expected to last.

A familiar tension crept into his shoulders as he studied the figures. He needed to work faster and find more streams of income. Every day that passed was another day where everything could fracture, and he still needed months to get everything into place.

A memory surfaced. The day he learned his lesson.

Kandahar Province, 2014. He was leading his unit on what should have been a routine patrol when the order came through to stand down. Some politician's backroom deal declared their sector stabilized despite clear intelligence warning of insurgent activity.

Within two hours, they watched helplessly as the village they'd been protecting was overrun.

Screams echoed across the valley, along with the sound of gunfire and the thud of metal on flesh and bone.

When the orders finally came through to reengage, they entered the village to find ashes and blood and the brutalized corpses of women and children.

The system they trusted, the chain of command they believed in, had failed those people. Who else might it fail in the future?

Jack's hand moved unconsciously to the scar on his left shoulder, a souvenir from the firefight that followed as the attackers returned. His wound healed, but the lesson scarred much deeper.

Institutions would fail. Those in authority would fail. Even the most powerful military force in the world would fail.

Only the prepared would survive.

Jack returned home months later to a country he barely recognized. While he and his men fought in distant lands, rot had spread through the foundations of the USA. He saw it everywhere. The obesity epidemic, the homeless and illegal immigrant invasion, plummeting birth rates and gender confusion. The woke bullshit on mainstream media.

He had gone looking for answers and, one disturbed night, Jack had discovered a prepper forum online. Real men talking about preparations for the civil war they knew must come, when they would fight for the land of the free like their ancestors had done.

Their discussion and warnings resonated with everything Jack had learned the hard way. These men understood. They saw the signs. Their discussions of bug-out locations and survival strategies gave form to his restless energy, and he started to plan his own sovereign territory.

The Ozarks were perfect, with dense forest and defendable terrain. His compound would be completely self-sufficient: solar power, greenhouse, weapons and ammunition stations, a medical bay. It would be a fortress against the coming storm.

But fortresses required capital to build.

The Sanctuary had seemed perfect when he found the job listing. A remote location with wealthy clients, minimal oversight, and a high salary. The perfect cover for his side ventures. The snake venom trade alone had added six figures to his fund over the last year.

And now, with Barclay's arrival, he would get another cash payout. Not much, but everything counted, and Jack intended to buy more Bitcoin with the promised funds. The only currency that would count when the economy tanked, as it inevitably would.

He switched over to the security feed in Barclay's room, one of the smaller, more affordable rooms at the hotel.

The writer paced up and down, his hands worrying at the strap of his leather messenger bag, which he still carried over his shoulder as if the contents were too precious to put down. Jack knew his type. Academics thought they were so superior, talking with bullshit big words, though they would just be food for carrion birds when disaster struck. But for now, they were good for dollars, so he'd take the money and not give Barclay another thought.

Jack stood and checked the blueprints he had assembled from county records at the writer's request. He had uncovered some maps that Tara had clearly tried to bury, presumably for planning reasons. Tunnels honeycombed the bedrock beneath the Sanctuary, but they had been sealed off during construction. Barclay claimed to need exact plans so his book was realistic, but Jack had a suspicion there might be more to it.

He headed out of his office and passed a group of staff members rushing to fix another AC malfunction.

They nodded respectfully at their security chief. As they should.

Jack reached Barclay's door, the blueprint tucked securely under his arm.

He rapped twice with sharp military precision.

Inside, something clattered. Probably Barclay hiding whatever he'd been looking at. Amateur move.

"Who is it?" The writer's voice carried a tremor of anxiety.

"Security." Jack kept his tone neutral, professional. "With the information you requested."

A pause, then footsteps.

The door opened just enough to reveal Barclay's flushed face. His eyes darted to the blueprint before meeting Jack's gaze.

"Yes, yes, come in." He stepped back, opening the door wider. "I was just reviewing my research."

Jack entered like a predator crossing into unfamiliar territory, every sense alert.

A sheaf of papers and a couple of old books lay on the desk, their spines cracked and pages marked with colored tabs. Jack almost scoffed at the waste of precious time, but managed to restrain himself. Just get the money.

He had seen Barclay's type in Afghanistan. Soft-handed academics who thought their PhDs and research grants gave them a special insight into warfare and survival. They arrived fresh-faced with theories and surveys, eager to document and understand what men like Jack really lived through.

Most lasted only a few weeks before the reality of blood and sand and war sent them scurrying back to their ivory towers.

Barclay's laptop displayed a half-written paper about Spanish missions and an open browser page. All that knowledge at his fingertips, and still no clue how to survive in the real world. When the grid went down, when the internet disappeared, all these books and theories would be mere kindling.

But for now, Jack was happy enough to take advantage of Barclay's desperation for local knowledge.

The writer's email had been specific. Hotel architectural blueprints in exchange for cash, the kind of side deal Jack had run dozens of times.

He had originally thought the writer's interest purely intellectual, but now he was here, something in the writer's demeanor and the intensity behind his scholarly facade suggested this might be far more than just academic research.

Jack recognized the hunger in Barclay's eyes. He had seen the same look on men about to do something risky, something dangerous.

That kind of desperation could be useful, if properly channeled. Like the snakes in the terrarium, Barclay might serve multiple purposes before outliving his usefulness.

Jack spread the blueprints out across the table in the living area. Desert light filtered through gauzy curtains, casting the architectural drawings in a sepia glow that made them look ancient.

Barclay's hands trembled slightly as they hovered over the paper, not quite touching it. His eagerness leaked from him like blood in the water.

"You asked for detailed plans." Jack traced a path with one finger, following ghostly lines of long-buried passages. "These tunnels were sealed off during construction. I've not been down in the area. There's been no need."

Barclay leaned closer to the blueprint, and the stink of his cheap aftershave and nervous sweat wafted over the table. "What about camera coverage in these areas?"

"Limited." Jack tapped specific points on the blueprint. "Blind spots here, here, and here. Maintenance access only, so there was no need for further security. Unless you feel the area requires closer attention?"

"No, no, of course not." Barclay pulled a leather-bound notebook from his messenger bag, its pages dog-eared and stuffed with loose papers. "This is only research for my book on the Spanish missions in the region. Religious purposes only, of course. There's evidence of an original mission below these foundations, but I'm sure nothing of any value was kept here." He hesitated. "Unless, of course, something has been found? Or reported locally?"

"I haven't heard anything." Jack kept his face neutral, though his pulse quickened. This was the real reason behind Barclay's academic interest.

The pulsing of a vein on his temple, the sheen of sweat on his brow despite the air conditioning, the waver in his voice. The writer knew something.

Other Spanish missions had kept gold and precious objects. Who knows what might be beneath the Sanctuary?

Jack walked to the window and looked out at the vastness of the desert. How many others had walked here over centuries, plotting to extract wealth from this unforgiving land? The weak ones died in the attempt. The smart ones used others to do the dangerous work for them.

Barclay shuffled through his notes. "Of course, I wouldn't expect anything to be found. These plans are just for my academic research. Historical documentation for my next book. All for local color. Nothing important."

He was talking too much. Clearly nervous chatter.

Jack returned to the table, deliberately invading the writer's personal space. "The Sanctuary takes its role as custodian of this site seriously. Any unauthorized access to these areas would be… problematic."

Barclay swallowed. "Naturally. I wouldn't dream of trying to investigate further." A beat of silence. "But hypothetically, if one were to discover items of historical significance?"

"Hypothetically," Jack echoed, "such discoveries could be handled with discretion. To protect the site's integrity, of course."

The writer's breathing grew shallow, his excitement barely contained, and Jack wondered what the hell Barclay had discovered in his old books.

"If I were to ask for permission to explore, I could provide additional documentation to back up my research," Barclay offered, his words tumbling out faster now. "Historical context, maps from the period — and extra payment, of course."

Jack tapped the blueprint with precise movements. "Don't go exploring on your own. Those old tunnels can be unstable. Accidents can happen down there."

"Of course, of course." Barclay's hands fluttered like the wings of a trapped bird. "If you're concerned about safety, perhaps we could arrange some kind of joint exploration?"

A wolfish smile touched Jack's lips as he calculated scenarios. The writer was practically gift-wrapping himself. "I'll consider it."

Jack's watch vibrated. Time for another security sweep.

Barclay could wait for now, but the man's rapid breathing as Jack turned to leave and the rustle of papers as the writer returned to his research, all indicated that he would try something soon. The only question was when.

CHAPTER 8

CASEY STOOD AT THE edge of Artists Palette, the painted hills rising behind her. As Rafael gave Isla an anatomy lesson and Grace took more photos, Casey turned away from her guests, a frown on her face.

The morning's crystal clarity had shifted.

Something was wrong.

The wind that had been pushing steadily from the east suddenly died, leaving an unnatural stillness that made her skin prickle.

Then it changed direction entirely, bringing a chill that had no place in Death Valley.

Movement caught her eye. A pair of ravens wheeled sharply against the sky, fleeing eastward. What had sparked their flight?

She turned to the west.

The Panamint Range should have been clearly visible, its peaks sharp against the horizon. Instead, they had vanished behind a wall of red-brown darkness that reached from the desert floor all the way up into the clouds.

The storm front boiled upward like a living thing, its leading edge churning with violent motion. Savage updrafts ripped desert scrub from the valley floor and tore it apart to be absorbed into the maelstrom. Ascending layers of sand moved in impossible patterns: demonic faces reaching out with clawed hands and animal spirits that quickly dissolved back into chaos.

Through her time in Death Valley, Casey had seen dust storms before. The locals called them *haboobs*, walls of sand and dust created when thunderstorm downdrafts hit the desert floor.

But this was something else entirely.

It was gigantic. And it would be on them in minutes.

The storm moved fast, demolishing everything in its path. It ripped up small trees, obliterating the careful lines of the park service roads, and transformed the familiar terrain into an alien landscape of churning sand and shadow.

Lightning flickered deep within the mass, brief strokes of purple-white that illuminated the layers of sand from within. The thunder that followed was almost subsonic, more felt than heard, vibrating in her bones.

They were too far from the hotel. Too exposed.

The dune buggy suddenly felt absurdly fragile.

Casey pushed away the primal fear that had frozen her. They had maybe ten minutes before the storm reached them.

Seven minutes to get down the switchback trail.

Another eight to cross the flats to the hotel.

The math didn't work, but they had to try.

"Everyone in the buggy!" she shouted. "Now! Move!"

"But I haven't finished my shot," Grace protested, still adjusting her phone's angle.

"Now!" Casey grabbed Isla's arm, practically lifting the girl into the passenger seat as Grace jumped into the back. "Rafael, let's go!"

The celebrity chef cursed but complied as the wind suddenly intensified, nearly knocking him off balance. Sand pelted their exposed skin like tiny needles as the edge of the storm reached them.

Casey jumped into the driver's seat, her hands finding

the wheel as muscle memory took over. The engine roared to life.

In the back mirror, she watched the storm devour the landscape. The sun dimmed to a sickly orange disk, its light struggling through the approaching wall of sand. The temperature plummeted, a good fifteen-degree drop in seconds.

Her fingers tightened on the wheel as she slammed the buggy into gear. "Hold on!" she shouted over the rising wind. She gunned the engine, tires spinning against the loose surface before finding purchase.

The storm was faster than she'd expected. Much faster.

Dark tendrils of sand chased them, reaching out like grasping fingers. The wind howled, drowning out Isla's frightened gasps from the passenger seat.

Casey took the first turn too fast, the buggy's wheels lifting slightly on the outside edge.

She corrected, fighting the vehicle's momentum, every muscle straining as she wrestled with the steering wheel.

Her mind flashed to the cave in the Mendips, to another moment when she'd been responsible for young lives. Not again. Never again.

"Nobody's dying today," she whispered as she blinked against the stinging sand, grateful for her sunglasses even as visibility dropped to nearly nothing.

The storm engulfed them just as they rounded the last bend to the hotel approach.

The world disappeared in a suffocating brown haze.

Casey drove purely by memory and the buggy shuddered as powerful gusts threatened to lift it off its wheels.

A flash of lightning split the sky, so close the thunder was instantaneous. The electrical discharge illuminated the storm in strobing violence, transforming the swirling sand into sheets of ghostly purple-white.

"There!" Isla shouted, pointing through the maelstrom.

The hotel's outline emerged from the chaos, and Casey

aimed for it, her arms aching from fighting the sideways shear.

The wind was a living thing now, trying to tear the buggy apart around them. Sand found every gap in their clothing, working its way into eyes, nose, mouth. She could taste it, metallic and ancient on her tongue.

The main hotel entrance appeared suddenly through the storm. Casey braked hard to avoid overshooting, and the buggy slid sideways before grinding to a halt.

Together, they stumbled from the vehicle.

The wind nearly knocked Isla off her feet. Casey grabbed her arm, keeping her upright as they staggered toward the entrance.

The hotel's windows visibly vibrated, the glass flexing under the storm's assault as sand scoured every exposed surface.

The automatic doors whooshed open, admitting them into the artificial calm of the lobby. The contrast was jarring. Outside, nature raged unchecked. Inside, the air conditioning hummed placidly, maintaining its artificial bubble of civilization.

Casey did a quick headcount. Isla, Grace, Rafael. All present, all whole, if somewhat sandblasted. Her hands shook slightly as the adrenaline ebbed.

Rafael spun toward her. "You should have seen that storm coming. How the hell am I meant to get any footage now?"

He stomped off, swearing under his breath.

By the window, Grace swayed on her feet and put a hand against the glass. "We almost died out there," she whispered, pulling out her phone to take photos. The look on her face suggested that this would be turned into some kind of spectacular content — and for once, Casey couldn't blame the influencer's instincts. The storm was certainly dramatic.

Through the lobby's vast windows, Casey watched it consume their world. The buggy disappeared from view, swallowed by the swirling brown mass. Lightning flashed, each strike highlighting the sheets of airborne sand in stark relief.

"Casey?" Isla's voice broke through her thoughts. "Are we safe now?"

Casey looked down at the girl, seeing the trust in her eyes. "We're inside. That's what matters for now."

But as the storm hammered against the windows, Casey knew they weren't safe. Not really. They could only retreat to a fragile bubble of civilization, pretending they were in control. Perhaps today they could keep the desert out, but the Sanctuary, like any human creation, could only ever be temporary in this brutal place.

As they stood watching, guests and staff alike emerged from various parts of the hotel, drawn to the spectacle outside as the lobby became an impromptu gathering place.

The vast windows that normally showcased Death Valley's stark beauty now displayed an apocalyptic scene. The storm's violence made the glass flex and bend, creating distortions that turned the whirling sand into nightmarish shapes. Every few seconds, lightning illuminated the chaos, casting strange shadows across the polished limestone floor.

"Is this normal?" a woman in designer yoga gear asked. "I mean, they would have warned us if—"

"My flight's supposed to leave tomorrow," another guest interrupted. "They can't possibly—"

"The internet's patchy," someone called out from near the reception desk. "My signal keeps going in and out."

Casey recognized a rising pitch of panic in their voices. She'd heard it before when people first realized how far they were from help, and the lobby's temperature-controlled air suddenly felt too thin.

"The storm is interfering with satellite communications," Tara's calm voice cut through the murmurs as she descended the lobby's curved staircase, moving with practiced grace, each step measured.

Casey had to admire the timing. Tara knew exactly when to make her entrance.

"My dear guests," Tara continued, coming to rest on the third step up, high enough to command the room without towering over those gathered. "You are witnessing one of Death Valley's most dramatic natural spectacles. This storm, while impressive, is a completely normal part of the desert's weather patterns."

Lightning flashed, making the windows rattle ominously. Several guests jumped.

Tara waited for the thunder to pass before speaking again, letting the storm punctuate her words.

"The Desert Sanctuary was specifically designed to withstand these conditions. Our walls are reinforced with the same materials used in hurricane zones. The windows are specially engineered to flex rather than break."

Casey wondered if that was really true. She had heard some of the local workers talk about the corners cut during construction, inferior materials clad with veneers to keep up appearances, and unpaid bills, of which her invoices were some of many. But Tara's confidence was almost enough to make her doubt the rumors.

"We have comprehensive backup systems, and enough supplies to keep everyone more than comfortable until the storm passes."

The crowd's energy shifted, their shoulders relaxing. Nervous laughter replaced fearful whispers as Tara reframed the crisis as an exclusive experience. Not a disaster, but a luxury adventure with five-star catering.

"Think of this as an opportunity and don't wish the time away." Tara gestured to the maelstrom outside. "After all, how many people can say they've witnessed the raw power of Death Valley from such a privileged vantage point? Make the most of it, and of course, we have much more for you to enjoy. Our chef has prepared a special menu for this evening's banquet. The spa is offering complimentary storm-watching massages. And our theater will show a curated selection of films if you'd prefer a different kind of thriller."

As Tara charmed the gathered guests, Casey noticed Jack standing across the lobby in his usual corner, his expression unreadable. But something in his stance set off warning bells in her head. He was too still, too focused on the storm, almost as if he anticipated disaster.

"Now, I suggest you all return to your rooms and freshen up," Tara concluded. "Consider this nature's invitation to unplug and embrace the luxury of isolation. Our staff are here to make this unexpected adventure as comfortable as possible."

The guests dispersed, their fears soothed by Tara's practiced performance. But Casey saw how the owner's fingers worried at her silk sleeve when she thought no one was watching, the tiny tell betraying uncertainty.

Outside, the storm continued its assault.

Sand piled up against the glass in drifts, only to be torn away by the next violent gust. The sun was completely obscured now, turning the day into an eerie twilight broken only by lightning.

Casey felt the vibrations through the floor, not just from the wind, but from the hotel's air conditioning straining to maintain the artificial environment. How long would the filters cope with this level of particulate matter? How long before the desert found its way inside?

The Mendip caves had taught her you could use all the safety equipment, follow every protocol, but in the end, humans, with all their technological defenses, were still just fragile flesh and bone.

As the last guests left, Tara remained standing on her step like a captain at the helm of a ship, staring out at the storm.

As Casey turned to leave, a large piece of desert rock thudded into the glass, and she thought she saw Tara's mask slip. Genuine fear flashed across the owner's face, quickly hidden.

Casey knew what it meant to be responsible for lives in the face of nature's indifference and as she turned and walked away, she looked down at her hands, still gritty with sand. The desert was already inside, carried in on their clothes, in their hair. In their lungs. How much further would it advance today?

CHAPTER 9

As the last of the guests and staff left the lobby, Tara remained, unable to tear her gaze from the maelstrom outside.

The vast atrium felt different now, transformed from a showpiece of luxury into something more ominous. The glass dome above groaned under the storm's assault. She forced herself to stand still, projecting calm even though her heart thundered against her ribs.

"The glass isn't rated for this level of wind shear." Jack's voice came from behind her, measured and clinical. The man moved like a predator and she hadn't heard him approach.

Tara kept her eyes on the storm, not giving him the satisfaction of startling her. "The engineering specs were within tolerance."

"For normal conditions, plus or minus ten percent." He moved to stand beside her. "Even for Death Valley, you know this isn't normal."

Through the windows, the sand moved in impossible patterns, in a twilight broken only by lightning flashes that turned the swirling debris into abstract nightmares.

Tara remained silent.

"I've mapped four evacuation routes." Jack's stance was military-rigid, his tone clipped. "The northwest exit is already compromised. Sand's piling up faster than maintenance can clear it. The east wing's backup generator is showing strain. If the main power fails—"

"It won't fail." The words came out sharper than Tara intended.

A violent gust made the glass dome flex. Fine sand sifted through some microscopic gap, drawing a line across the floor like a warning.

"I've read your contingency reports," Tara said, smoothing her dress with perfectly manicured fingers. "The shelter areas, the supply caches, the backup communications. All very thorough, and of course, we will use them if necessary. But this storm will be over soon. There is no need to overreact."

Tara knew more about Jack than his official resume. The psychological evaluations from his military discharge. The pattern of short-term security contracts, each ending abruptly. The survivalist forums he frequented. Jack Abrams was a man preparing for the end of the world. That was part of why she'd hired him, but it also made him prone to catastrophic thinking.

"The guests will need to be moved from the east wing," he continued. "The structural integrity—"

"The guests will remain exactly where they are, enjoying the unique experience of witnessing Death Valley's raw power from the comfort of luxury."

Lightning flashed, casting their reflections against the dark glass.

"You're thinking like a soldier," she said, softening her tone. "I need you to think like the head of security for a five-star resort. These people paid for an exclusive desert experience. We're simply providing a more, let's say, dramatic experience than advertised."

Jack's jaw tightened. "And if things get worse?"

"Then we'll implement your contingencies." She turned

to face him. "But until that moment, we maintain the illusion that everything is fine. That's what they're paying for. That's what I'm paying you for."

She saw the calculation in Jack's eyes, his military mind mapping threats and responses. But there were things he didn't know, couldn't know. Things he wouldn't need to know if the storm passed quickly.

"Yes, ma'am," he said finally, conveying a lack of respect even with his polite tone. "I'll monitor the stress points. But I recommend moving emergency supplies to the central storage area. Just in case your illusion needs… reinforcement."

Tara nodded, a precise tilt of her head that dismissed him without words.

He walked away, leaving her alone with the storm.

Only when his footsteps had faded completely did she allow herself to exhale and release the tension in her shoulders. Jack was good at his job. Perhaps too good.

The storm howled against the windows, and Tara lifted her chin, facing it with the same determination that had carried her from poverty to this moment. She had built her life on turning disaster into opportunity, and this would be no different.

She just had to maintain control a little longer and keep the carefully constructed facade from crumbling until she secured the investments she needed. Maxwell Carver-Scott, or perhaps Grace Lin's father. Both were on her list to pitch for investment. She was confident they would be impressed by the experience of nature offered at the Desert Sanctuary over the coming days. The storm could be reframed as a unique and authentic encounter with nature. Something billionaires paid handsomely for.

The glass dome rattled once more, but Tara didn't flinch. She had buried her fears too deep for even this storm to unearth them.

Or so she hoped.

She turned from the storm and made her way up to her office. Each step in her high heels was controlled, even though no one was watching. The habit of perfection was too deeply ingrained to break.

Tara closed her office door behind her with a soft click, and only then did she allow her shoulders to drop.

She pressed her forehead against the cool wood of the door, breathing in the familiar scent of sage and cedar from the traditional smudging she performed each morning. It was a private ritual connecting her to her roots, to her father's Timbisha Shoshone family, even as she played the role of luxury hotelier in public.

"Breathe," she whispered, the word catching in her throat. "Just breathe."

But the hotel's dire finances flashed through her mind like warning lights. The food deliveries that now couldn't arrive, the dwindling supplies, the massive utility bills that just about kept the desert at bay. She couldn't afford whatever damage this storm might bring or the potential PR disaster that would stop others from coming here.

Tara crossed to the bookshelf, her fingers finding the hidden catch that released a false panel. Behind it, packets of classic Oreos piled up. Her secret shame, her private weakness, and the only thing that could help her feel better right now.

She selected a packet and returned to her desk. The wrapper crinkled in her trembling hands as she tore it open.

Her laptop screen cast a harsh glow as she pulled up the week's schedule. The carefully planned events read like a joke. Sunrise yoga, stargazing, locally guided hikes. All impossible in these conditions.

But it was the potential lost investment opportunities that concerned her the most.

"Maxwell Carver-Scott, net worth 4.2 billion," she

murmured, clicking through his file. "Grace Lin, daughter of Richard Lin, real estate portfolio valued at 1.8 billion." The numbers blurred as she blinked back tears of frustration. This was meant to be a glorious few days that would lead to investment, expansion, acclaim.

She bit into an Oreo, letting the sweetness fill her mouth. Her mother's voice, stern but loving, rang in her ears. 'Tara girl, you can't eat your feelings away.'

But she had been eating them and transforming them into fuel for her ambition since she was a child growing up in the shadow of these same mountains.

Her father had been Timbisha, her mother a local from near Las Vegas, and together they eked out a living here in the tourist industry while Tara was young.

The desert had been both backdrop and teacher, showing her how to appear harsh and unbending while nurturing secret wells of strength deep below the surface.

When an accident maimed her father and the health insurance wouldn't pay enough to manage his pain, he spiraled into depression, dying by suicide when she was just fifteen.

Her mother was still alive, but now estranged from her daughter. Tara thought of her sometimes, but she knew it was for the best they no longer kept in touch. She had spent years sloughing off what held her back; returning here as an owner, as a boss, justified all her life choices.

Tara pulled up the building's maintenance logs, her heart sinking as she reviewed the compromises she'd been forced to make during construction.

The reinforced glass was grade B, not A. The backup generators were refurbished, not new. Each corner cut had seemed necessary at the time, each risk calculated against the dwindling budget.

"Just hold together," she whispered, as much to herself as to the building. "Please."

She thought of the sealed-off section beneath the hotel, the ancient mission ruins discovered during the initial survey. The archaeologists had been excited, talking about preservation and historical significance. But Tara had seen only delays, regulations, oversight. All the things that could have killed her dream before it began.

She had buried the reports along with the ruins and built her future on top of it.

She munched another Oreo as she reviewed the inventory lists. Three days of food at normal consumption rates, maybe five if they rationed carefully. The water recycling system was robust, at least. They could survive this storm, and she would rebuild any damage. There was always another chance.

But the chocolate turned bitter in her mouth as she remembered her father's words. 'The desert gives, and the desert takes. You can't build permanence on shifting sand.'

But she had tried. How she had tried.

Every detail of the Desert Sanctuary had been chosen to create an illusion of humanity's triumph over nature. The hidden drip systems coaxing the native plants in the gardens to bloom frequently, the pools maintained at a perfect temperature, the air itself scrubbed and cooled and scented to match her exacting standards.

All of it dependent on systems that could fail, on supplies that could run out, on a thousand delicate balances she maintained through sheer force of will.

Her fingers shook as she reached for another Oreo.

Just one more, she promised herself. Just one more, and then she would be strong again.

She could put the mask of the capable hotelier back on. She would figure out how to turn this disaster into an exclusive experience that her wealthy guests would want to post about, brag about. Invest in.

A notification popped up on her screen.

A guest complaint about the Wi-Fi. Then another about their jacuzzi water pressure. Another about the availability of a certain wine.

Outside her window, the storm had turned the afternoon to night, broken only by flashes of lightning that illuminated the swirling sand. Each flash seemed to count down to something, though Tara didn't want to think about what.

She could almost feel the weight of the desert pressing against the glass, searching for weaknesses, for a way in.

Her manicured fingernail traced the edge of the keyboard as she contemplated her next move.

The hotel's network infrastructure display glowed on her screen. It was a complex web of connections that usually kept her guests tethered to the outside world.

Their digital lifelines.

Their power to destroy everything she had built with a single poor review or viral post.

"Not today," she whispered.

With three precise keystrokes, she disabled the main Wi-Fi router. Four more commands severed the backup connections. The external phone lines were next. A simple matter of rerouting them through a storm-damaged junction box.

The system status lights on her screen turned red one by one. In rooms throughout the hotel, phones would go dead, Wi-Fi signals would disappear.

Soon the complaints would increase in volume, but she was ready. She would blame the storm, and who could argue with nature's fury? She would spin it as the ultimate digital detox, something to be treasured, something others would crave. If she could control the narrative, she might just emerge from this unscathed, even triumphant.

Her hand trembled slightly as she reached for the last Oreo and finished it in two bites, even though the sweetness was now cloying, the edge of shame now tainting the familiar pleasure.

Enough of this weakness.

Tara shut her laptop with a decisive click and walked into her private bathroom, her heels clicking against the marble floor.

The space was as meticulously designed as every other inch of her hotel. Gleaming surfaces, perfect lighting, luxury toiletries arranged with geometric precision. Her reflection greeted her from multiple angles, each mirror positioned to ensure she never had a flaw unchecked.

Tara placed a towel on the floor tiles and knelt in front of the toilet, her silk dress rustling.

The ritual was familiar. Two fingers pressed just so. Her throat contracted, muscles in a practiced dance of control. The cookies came up easily, her body as obedient as her staff.

Tears pricked at her eyes. From the effort, she told herself, not emotion. Never emotion.

Tara flushed away the evidence of her weakness, watching the water swirl until every trace was gone.

At the sink, she washed her hands with mechanical precision, using the luxury hand soap she'd personally selected for its subtle blend of desert sage and citrus. The scent grounded her, reminding her of who she was, of what she had built — and what was at stake.

Her toothbrush was perfectly aligned in its holder, waiting. The motions were automatic. Rinse, brush, rinse again, as the mint taste erased all evidence of weakness.

Tara leaned closer to the mirror and examined her reflection with a professional eye as she reapplied her lipstick. The shade was called Desert Rose, custom-made to match the exact color of the mineral deposits in the cliffs outside. Every detail mattered.

"The banquet," she reminded her reflection, adjusting her silk dress so it draped just right. "Focus on the banquet."

It would be her masterstroke. Let the storm rage while her guests dined on exquisitely plated courses, drank rare wines, and forgot their disconnection from the outside world.

Tara straightened her spine and rolled her shoulders back, feeling the familiar mask of control settle into place. She lifted her chin. Minor adjustments that transformed her into Tara Jensen, owner of the exclusive Desert Sanctuary.

A final check in the mirror. Her lipstick was perfect, her eyes bright but not too bright, her face composed but not rigid. The mask was complete.

The bathroom light flickered. Just for a moment, but enough to make her heart stutter.

The backup generators should prevent any outages, but even they had their limits. Just as she did.

"Not yet," she told the flickering light. "Hold together. Just a little longer."

Tara took one final, deep breath, letting it out slowly through perfectly painted lips. Then she opened the bathroom door and headed back out, ready to face her staff, her guests. The storm itself.

Let them all come. She had not fought her way up from nothing to be defeated now. Not by the desert, not by bankruptcy, not by her own weaknesses.

The banquet would be a triumph. She would make sure of it.

She had to.

CHAPTER 10

GRACE STOOD AT THE floor-to-ceiling windows of her suite, still wearing the sand-dusted hiking gear from their terrifying buggy ride back to the hotel. Her hands trembled slightly as she raised her phone, seeking the perfect angle despite her rattled nerves.

Outside, the storm transformed the panoramic windows into a canvas, sand and darkness swirling together like an abstract painting come to life. The desert felt different from in here, separated by inches of glass from the forces that had nearly killed them less than an hour ago, but Grace wanted to keep the edge of danger alive.

"Hey, loves," she breathed into her phone's camera, letting genuine fear bleed into her usually practiced voice. "I'm coming to you from Death Valley, where we're literally being swallowed by a massive storm."

She panned slowly to show the wall of sand battering the windows. "The wind sounds like…" she paused, remembering how it had shrieked around the dune buggy, "…like the desert is screaming."

It was a perfect line imbued with genuine emotion, and Grace expected it would be shared and remixed and shared again as the viral video caught the algorithms.

She hit Post. Nothing happened.

The loading wheel spun endlessly.

She switched to back up cellular data. Nothing. Her personal hotspot. Dead.

"No, no, no." She jabbed frantically at different apps with increasing urgency. TikTok, Instagram, even X — all refused to connect.

She was truly alone. Cut off from the world. What the hell was she meant to do now?

The luxury suite's pristine white furniture and minimalist décor suddenly felt suffocating. Like every other gilded cage her father had placed her in, the Swiss boarding school, the Manhattan penthouse, the carefully controlled internships working on his company's most prestigious projects. All designed to keep her safe, contained — and cut off from reality.

Her whole life had been one cushioned room after another, protecting her from any real consequence or challenge. Her influencer status on social media was the one thing she truly controlled, and her followers knew who she really was. Unlike her family.

Grace pressed her forehead against the cool glass of the window, feeling the vibration of the wind's assault. She was eight years old again, watching another kind of storm approach. Lawyers and reporters swarmed their Hong Kong penthouse as her father's first company imploded. She remembered his face as he stood at windows just like these, watching his empire crumble.

It was only temporary, and he'd rebuilt, of course. Richard Lin always rebuilt, bigger and stronger than before.

But she'd cried in front of the cameras that day, and he had never looked at her in the same way again.

"Weakness is unforgivable," he said. "The Lin name means strength."

As he turned away, she heard the words he muttered to her mother. The words that shaped her future: "We'd better have a boy next."

And they had. Perfect Michael, with his Stanford MBA and his instinct for the family business. Michael, who never posted on social media because he was 'too busy with real work.' Who would inherit all the Lin businesses while she was considered too frivolous to be trusted with anything important.

But the storm had shown Grace something out there in the desert.

She wasn't as weak as they all thought. She had faced real danger, felt genuine fear, and survived. Her designer clothes and carefully curated posts were just another kind of armor, hiding the steel beneath.

They all underestimated her. Her father, her brother, even the eco-collective she had joined who thought she was just another trust fund fraud. Today's storm crystallized something inside of her, burning away the last traces of uncertainty. She would not be Richard Lin's disappointing daughter anymore. She would make a real impact. The world would notice — and so would her father.

Lightning flashed through the swirling sand, illuminating Grace's reflection in the window. She barely recognized herself. Windblown, dusty, her eyes bright with purpose rather than her usual calculated charm. Good. It was time to become someone new, someone who did more than just document the world through a perfect filter. She would become the kind of story other people posted about.

A memory of the board meeting last year rose unbidden. Michael's perfectly tailored suit, his Stanford MBA confidence, as he sneered at her concerns about the ecological impact of the company's latest developments.

"You're just playing at activism, Gracie. Why don't you stick to posting pretty pictures? Leave the real work to people who get their hands dirty doing real business."

She tried to protest, to explain about water rights and the effect on indigenous land.

Michael just laughed. "The profit margins more than offset any environmental impact and government fines."

Grace fled the gleaming corporate headquarters that day, her face burning with humiliation. Eventually, she found herself in a small coffee shop in a part of San Francisco her father would never countenance visiting.

The barista had radical climate change slogans tattooed on her arms and a knowing look in her eyes as Grace posted shots of her coffee art. "You're Richard Lin's daughter, right? The influencer?"

Instead of the usual fawning, there had been a challenge in the young woman's voice. "Ever wonder how many species die every time Daddy builds another luxury resort?"

"I do wonder, which is why I just got kicked out of a board meeting for warning them about the consequences."

That conversation led to more, and then to underground meetings where activists spoke passionately about direct action and systemic change.

They had been suspicious of her at first. But Grace had proven herself, using her social media skills to spread their message and her insider knowledge to warn them about upcoming developments.

Her hands shook as she pulled up the encrypted messaging app, the one her father's security team would never approve of, the one that connected her to people who knew that sometimes you had to break things to fix them.

The last message received before her trip glowed on the screen. "Time to prove yourself. The package we sent has everything you need. Don't let us down, princess."

Grace frowned at the mocking nickname, but she understood its purpose. The eco-collective never let her forget her privilege, and unlike the sycophants in her father's world, the activists challenged her, pushed her to be better, to do more. Today, she would prove she was worth their trust.

She retrieved her sustainable hemp and bamboo luggage

from the wardrobe and slipped open a side zip. Inside, wrapped in brown paper and recycled padding, lay a packet of innocent-looking granules.

The eco-collective chemist had explained that the compound would react with the water system's industrial chemicals, turning the hotel's pristine pools into black sludge. It would eventually overwhelm the filtration system with evidence of the Sanctuary's environmental shortcuts — and make for some epic images against the backdrop of the desert.

Grace weighed the granules in her hand. They were heavier than she expected, almost weighted with possibility. The storm presented an ideal opportunity to complete her mission while staff were distracted, and by the time it passed, the resulting scandal would be impossible to ignore. The Sanctuary's environmental violations would be exposed, and it would encourage the media to investigate all the other companies exploiting the desert for their own gain.

Including her father's companies.

Grace thought of the indigenous lands he and her brother had acquired. The diverted water rights, the disrupted ecosystems. All in the name of profit.

It was time to stop playing at being an influencer and truly change opinion. She would show her father, her brother — the world — that true strength meant standing against everything you'd been raised to believe in.

She would become the storm and sweep them all away.

Grace opened the hotel's maintenance schematics on her phone, checking the precise directions provided by the eco-collective. Follow the red line past the laundry facility, through two security doors, to the water treatment hub. She noted the keypad codes they'd somehow obtained, though her pulse quickened at the thought of using them.

With one last deep breath, Grace headed out into the corridors of the hotel, moving with practiced confidence, the way she'd learned to walk into exclusive venues and VIP events. Head high, purpose in every step.

She entered the service area, another world compared to the hotel's luxury spaces, with exposed pipes overhead, industrial-grade flooring, and the ever-present hum of machinery keeping the desert at bay. But the storm penetrated even here, making the metal walls creak and groan.

A maintenance worker appeared around a corner, his uniform stained with sweat.

Grace's heart jumped, but her smile stayed perfect and professional. She'd learned the power of a smile in a thousand social media posts.

"I'm so sorry, miss." The man looked confused. "This is a restricted maintenance area. You shouldn't be back here."

Grace let out a practiced laugh, the same one she used in her sponsored content. Not fake, just cultivated. "Oh, thank goodness. I thought I was lost! I'm Grace Lin." She held out her hand, and the man wiped his hand on his uniform before shaking as Grace continued. "The hotel manager Tara Jensen approved my social media content about the hotel's sustainability initiatives. The storm is actually the perfect backdrop to showcase your water recycling system."

She pulled up her largest social media profile, making sure the man could see the verified checkmark and her many millions of followers. "My audience is really interested in eco-tourism and sustainable luxury. Tara thought it would be great PR for the hotel. You can call her if you need to verify?"

The man hesitated, but Grace could see the respect for her influence in his eyes, and he clearly didn't want to bother his boss when things were so fraught with the storm.

"The system's under strain right now," he warned, but he was already stepping aside. "Please don't touch anything, okay? Just photos, right?"

"Of course!" Grace beamed. "I'll be quick. You're doing

amazing things here, by the way. The hotel's green initiatives are so impressive. Thank you for your hard work."

The worker smiled, ducking his head almost shyly before continuing down the corridor. Grace waited until his footsteps faded before letting her smile drop.

The water treatment room ahead hummed with technical efficiency as banks of monitors displayed flow rates and chemical levels.

Grace's hands trembled as she unwrapped the package. The granules looked harmless, like raw sugar or salt. Would this really be enough to do the job?

Her instructions were to check the size of the main water tanks and then adjust the amount she poured in based on that. But she didn't have time for calculations right now. She would just throw all of it in.

Grace found the main intake valve, just as the eco-collective had described. The metal was cool under her fingers as she opened an access panel.

Water rushed below, carrying thousands of gallons of precious desert resources through the hotel's artificial veins.

"For all the species that died for this place," she whispered, tipping the granules in. "For all the waters diverted, all the habitats destroyed."

The reaction was almost instant. The clear water darkened as threads of black spread like ink.

Grace pulled out her phone and recorded it with shaking hands.

"Phase one complete," she narrated softly, documenting the spreading contamination for her future audience once she was back online. "The hotel's environmental violations are about to become impossible to ignore."

Warning lights blinked on a nearby monitoring panel, shifting from a bank of solid green to a few flashes of yellow as the systems responded to the foreign substance.

Soon the lights would all be red and the pristine infinity

pools would turn black. Soon this hotel would be exposed for the environmental disaster it truly was.

Grace's heart pounded as she closed the access panel and wiped away any trace of the granules. It was a faster reaction than she had expected and she needed to get clear before the system registered the full contamination.

Perhaps she wouldn't post that video after all. Maybe it was better to deny being involved.

She shoved the empty package deep into her pocket and hurried away. The service corridor seemed much longer on her way out, the industrial lights harsh and accusing. Each step echoed like a countdown. She forced herself to walk normally, fighting the urge to run. The worker might still be nearby. Anyone might see.

Grace kept her pace steady. She was just another influencer, just another privileged guest. Nothing to see here.

CHAPTER 11

As Barclay descended into the hotel basement, the musty air grew thicker with each step. Bare fluorescent bulbs above cast harsh shadows, so different from the mellow mood lighting of the floors above. His fingers traced the rough paper of the primary blueprint the security chief, Jack, had given him, its edges already softening from his nervous sweat.

Down here, he could still hear the storm — a low, constant rumble that seemed to come from the earth itself. While everyone up in the hotel, including Jack, was occupied by the storm, he had free range to investigate what might be left of the old mission.

The basement stretched out before him, a maze of utility rooms and storage areas. He oriented himself, turning until he could match the modern layout with Jack's marked-up blueprints and his own older map indicating the original mission foundations. They should be just beyond the north wall.

Barclay could hardly believe he'd made it this far. Just three months earlier, he'd been slouched in his cramped apartment, surrounded by the detritus of failed research projects. Empty coffee cups, sticky notes, and overdue rental notices all around him.

But one particular reference caught his eye and drew him out of his depressive ennui. A footnote in an obscure Spanish missionary's diary mentioned *oro sagrado*, sacred gold, transported to the Misión Nuestra Señora del Desierto, the Mission of Our Lady in the Desert.

Barclay cross-referenced the approximate coordinates with modern maps of the area, discovering the Desert Sanctuary, which looked as if it had been built right over the old mission. His years of writing sensationalized pseudo-history, of twisting archaeological facts into palatable conspiracy theories for a hungry audience, might all be over. And not a moment too soon, because he couldn't churn out that crap anymore.

This was a chance at a genuine discovery. It could change his career, even the course of his life.

It had been hard to restrain his enthusiasm, but he kept his discovery quiet, and now here he was. All he had to do was find whatever was left of the mission.

Barclay hefted up his backpack, heavy with tools, and made his way to the northernmost storage room.

Steel shelving units lined the walls, filled with spare linen and cleaning supplies in one section and canned food in the other.

Barclay put his pack down and ran his hands along the furthest concrete wall, feeling for any irregularities. According to the historical records, the mission's main chapel had stood not far from here, with an adjoining crypt and treasury behind.

The wall felt solid, unforgiving.

He stretched behind a shelving unit and felt a slight change in the wall's texture. A vertical seam in the wall, where something had been bricked over. Could it be a tunnel opening?

Barclay shifted supplies, reducing the weight so he could move the shelving. The sound of the storm masked any noise, but he still needed to work quickly.

The sledgehammer felt reassuring in his hands, its weight a promise of revelation. He had used it once before — and that didn't work out so well — but this time would be different.

His colleagues in academia had shunned him after the Peruvian scandal, their polite emails growing shorter, before stopping altogether. "You've gone too far, Turner," his university department head had intoned with annoying superiority. "There are lines we don't cross."

But sometimes, the only way to uncover the secrets of history was to break a few rules, and this time, Barclay was sure it would be worth it.

He braced himself and took a swing at the wall.

The first strike sent vibrations up his arms.

Another blow, and another. His breath came in short gasps, sweat rolling down his back despite the cool basement air.

Small chunks of concrete fell away, revealing older stone beneath.

He struck again, putting his entire weight behind the blow. There was a sudden yielding sensation, and the sledgehammer crashed through with unexpected force. The impact reverberated up his arms as chunks of stone and decades of dust cascaded to the floor.

Heart pounding, Barclay lowered his hammer and peered at the ragged hole. His flashlight beam cut through swirling particles to reveal darkness beyond — not the solid wall he half-expected, but empty space. He couldn't help a smile. He had been right all along.

The excitement of what might lie beyond drove him now, and Barclay kept striking, gradually widening the hole. He paused periodically to check his progress, brushing away debris and shining his flashlight into the growing gap.

The beam caught something beyond. Not just rough stone but worked masonry. The air that drifted through the opening carried the weight of centuries.

"There you are," he whispered, his voice trembling with excitement.

Barclay switched to his smaller tools, carefully widening the hole until it was large enough to squeeze through.

As he worked, his mind raced with possibilities.

The mission's records had been vague about what exactly had been stored in this place. Anything valuable the priests here had acquired would have been in transit to the more significant West Coast missions, but it was likely there were at least goblets or other religious vessels for the Eucharist. There were tantalizing mentions of other treasures, perhaps sacred objects transported from Spain, or artifacts that the Church wanted to keep hidden way out here in the desert.

The last chunks of stone fell away.

Barclay stood before the opening, his flashlight beam cutting through decades of undisturbed darkness.

He took a deep breath to steady himself.

This discovery, properly documented and excavated with precision, would restore his reputation. He could return to serious academic work, his name cleared by the very methods that had once tarnished it.

Barclay clambered through the hole into the darkness beyond.

An ancient stone tunnel stretched before him, rough walls glistening with seeping moisture.

The passage sloped downward at a gentle angle, each step taking him further from the hotel's perimeter.

Barclay folded the blueprint away and followed the older mission map, taking several turns where the tunnels branched off before widening into a vaulted chamber with a wooden door at the end. Its ancient timbers were warped and split, held together by rusted iron bands. It looked to be mesquite, native to the region and incredibly dense, resistant to rot, perhaps protecting what lay beyond for all these years.

His hands trembled as he pressed against the door. It resisted for a moment, then gave way with an agonized groan that echoed through the tunnel. The sound made him wince. It was too loud, even with the storm outside.

But he was too close to stop now. He walked inside.

Barclay swept his flashlight beam across the chamber and gasped, his academic detachment crumbling at the sight before him.

The room was an ossuary, housing a collection of bones displayed in the European style, a testimony to the dark underbelly of Spanish colonial expansion.

At one end of the room, hundreds of skulls were mortared into columns that stretched toward a low vaulted ceiling, their eye sockets dark and accusing. Between them, arm and leg bones formed intricate rosettes and crosses, a perversion of sacred geometry that spoke of careful planning rather than hasty burial.

But these were not peaceful dead.

Many of the skulls bore distinctive star-shaped fractures of execution — death by gunshot or blunt-force trauma. Others showed the pitting of advanced syphilis, the disease having eaten through bone like acid. The symptoms would have driven these people mad before death claimed them. Was this a plague pit of sorts?

Barclay explored further and found other artifacts amongst the bones. Iron manacles, their chains green with age, and fragments of leather whips, their metal tips oxidized black, lying coiled among femurs and vertebrae. These weren't just victims of disease. They were evidence of systematic brutality.

His flashlight caught a collection of smaller skulls. Children, dozens of them, their developing bones showing signs of malnutrition and violence. Native children, likely taken from their families in the name of salvation.

Barclay turned from the ancient dead. There was nothing

he could do for them now, except treat their remains with respect and try to bring their story to light.

But there was more to be explored down here.

The remains of what must have been the mission's library lay against the furthest wall, partially preserved by the desert's dry air. Perhaps they moved it all down here when the desert heat started to get too much. The shelves were partially collapsed, and the books were mostly crumbled to dust, but he recognized fragments of ecclesiastical text, with Latin phrases speaking of redemption even as the evidence of torture surrounded them.

A leather-bound volume caught his eye.

He carefully lifted it out, and a sheaf of parchment fell from its pages, covered in spidery Spanish script, a language he knew well.

Madre de Dios, the fever spreads. Brother Thomas speaks in tongues, says the devil walks among us. The natives we gathered for salvation now flee into the desert. Those we catch must be purified through pain, their souls saved even as their bodies bleed...

The text trailed off, but Barclay could guess that religious fervor combined with disease had turned this mission into a charnel house.

The friars themselves must have sealed it off, and the authorities erased it from their maps rather than acknowledge what had happened here.

As Barclay turned, his light caught movement. He gasped, but no, it was just shadows playing across a nearly complete skeleton pressed into an alcove.

Its position was unnatural, the bones arranged as if the person had been walled up alive, their hands raised in a final plea. A silver crucifix still hung around the cervical vertebrae, while the finger bones clutched a rosary of wooden beads, preserved by the arid air. The skull's jaw gaped in a silent scream.

Scattered personal effects lay around the skeleton's feet. A clay pot of dried ink, quill nibs green with oxidation, and a set of keys. This had been someone of authority. Perhaps the mission's leader, sealed away by his own followers as the madness spread.

No wonder the hotel management had suppressed all mention of this place. What luxury resort would want guests knowing that they swam and dined above a chamber of horrors?

But this historical atrocity made the find even more newsworthy, and Barclay could imagine the frenzy of reporters as he expounded on it all against the backdrop of luxury.

He had to get back upstairs and report this as soon as possible. The human remains, especially those of indigenous people, made it even more important to preserve the scene. He couldn't help but grin as he surveyed his discovery. This would certainly seal his reputation.

His flashlight caught a glint of gold among the bones. He walked closer and gasped as the light revealed a small hoard of objects.

Coins, gold crosses, and rosaries of silver and precious stones.

The beam from the flashlight trembled as he swept it across the chamber, revealing more treasures nestled among the bones. Gilded chalices, silver monstrances, jeweled reliquaries.

And there, against the far wall, a wooden chest. Its corners had crumbled to dust, but the lock and hinges were solid Spanish iron, built to last centuries.

The Spanish had brought more than just faith to this land, and whatever darkness had consumed them here, they'd clearly never sent their wealth back across the ocean.

Barclay approached the chest slowly, his footsteps leaving imprints in the dust.

He reached out.

The chest's lid was heavy, but it yielded to his pressure.

Inside, gold coins caught his light and threw it back a hundredfold. A dragon's hoard of Spanish doubloons, each one a fortune in itself, both historically priceless and worth a small fortune in raw gold.

Barclay reached out and picked one up.

The metal was cool against his fingers, the weight of it both less and more than he'd expected. The coin bore the face of Philip V of Spain, the date still crisp despite the centuries. 1723. This was more than just money. It was a direct connection to the past.

Barclay took a deep breath and exhaled slowly as he considered his options.

The good archaeologist in him, the scholar who once cared only for knowledge, knew he should document everything and leave this place untouched. It was a priceless historical site, a window into a dark chapter of colonial history at a newly discovered mission, thought lost to the desert.

Death Valley was a national park, and federal law prohibited removal of any finds. The US government would claim the gold. The local Timbisha Shoshone would be consulted about the indigenous remains, and would have some claim on the gold as reparations for their historical suffering.

Barclay's fingers tightened around the coin.

The proper procedure was clear. He must document everything, report it through official channels, and then let the authorities handle excavation and preservation. There would be endless meetings and territorial squabbles between universities, museums, and government agencies.

And where would he be in all of that?

A footnote, at best. A disgraced archaeologist lucky to get a mention in the acknowledgments of any publications.

The same academics who had shunned him after Peru would swoop in and claim authority. They'd pick over the bones like vultures and further their own careers off the back of his discovery. He would be pushed to the fringes and would once again have to churn out sensationalized paperbacks to pay his rent.

Unless...

Barclay played his flashlight beam across the gold once more, making it gleam like fire in the darkness. There was enough wealth here to fund decades of independent research. No more begging for grants, no more publisher deadlines. He could choose his own projects, and do real archaeology — on his own terms.

The empty eye sockets of hundreds of skulls looked down as Barclay reached for another coin, trying to ignore how the shadows shifted and danced in his peripheral vision.

A trick of the light, surely.

Just his conscience playing tricks, making the carefully arranged bones seem to move, to reach out...

The air shifted behind him, carrying a whisper of movement that wasn't just his imagination.

A voice cut through the darkness. "Well, isn't this interesting?"

Barclay's heart nearly stopped. His flashlight beam jerked wildly across the walls as he spun around. There, emerging from the darkness, was Jack.

CHAPTER 12

JACK STRODE INTO THE chamber, his boots crunching through the dust of centuries-old bones. The sound reminded him of walking through bombed-out buildings in Kandahar, the same crackle of pulverized debris, the same weight of history reduced to rubble beneath his feet. His tactical flashlight cut through the darkness, throwing harsh shadows across the walls.

Barclay startled at his entrance, his eyes wide, open-mouthed as he let the gold coins slip from his fingers.

Satisfaction curled in Jack's gut. He had timed his entrance perfectly, letting the writer explore just far enough before making his move. Security cameras had monitored Barclay's discovery of the false wall in the storage room, and his work in opening the old tunnel and then leaving footprints in the dust to show the way certainly made Jack's life easier.

"I- I can explain," Barclay stammered, backing away. His heel caught on a fallen skull, sending it skittering across the floor. "This is a significant historical discovery. The mission records suggest—"

"Spare me the lecture." Jack bent and scooped up a handful of coins from the chest, letting them cascade through his fingers with the soft clink of metal on metal.

The sound of freedom.

With this kind of wealth, he could build a better-equipped compound. An underground bunker, solar arrays, ammunition stockpiles. Enough supplies to outlast any catastrophe. With these resources, he wouldn't just survive what was coming. He would be a leader in the new world that would emerge from the ashes of the old.

Jack traced the beam of his light over the artifacts scattered amongst the bones.

Chalices and reliquaries studded with gold and gems, their value astronomical even without the historical significance. He calculated practical matters: weight, portability, current market prices for melted-down precious metals. Perhaps he could even find a market in Mexico for the religious stuff. The collectors down there loved that shit.

Tara had to know about this place. There was no way this could have stayed hidden during construction. With her local contacts, she must have buried it, just like she buried anything that threatened her precious hotel's reputation.

He could use that against her. She wouldn't dare stop him taking the gold out of here.

"We must document this properly," Barclay said with academic authority. "The historical implications alone—"

"Here's what's going to happen." Jack took a step closer, crowding the smaller man's space. "We'll take what we can and split it evenly. The storm will give us cover later tonight. I can get it out in a maintenance truck and fence it from Vegas."

Jack saw the conflict play out across Barclay's face in a war of greed versus professional ethics. Jack had seen that same look in Afghanistan, watching supposedly upright men compromise their principles for significant gain, especially when no one would ever know.

"But the indigenous remains," Barclay protested weakly. "The historical context—"

"The bones aren't going anywhere. You can always report them later. Be the savior of these ancient dead." Jack dropped his voice lower. "But this gold? It's leaving with me tonight, so make your choice."

Barclay's shoulders slumped.

Victory. Jack could almost taste it, like gun metal on his tongue.

"How can we even move it all?" Barclay asked. "There's too much for us to carry."

"We'll be selective." Jack swept his flashlight across the chamber. "Focus on the highest value pieces first. The storm gives us maybe six to ten hours of cover before anyone can even respond to an emergency call, and we'll be long gone by then."

He was already categorizing the treasure in his mind with military precision. Portable versus unwieldy, historically identifiable versus anonymous, easily converted to cash versus requiring special buyers. Old habits died hard, and Jack had run enough tactical operations to know that success lay in making hard choices as fast as possible.

The ancient door creaked behind them, making Barclay jump.

It was just the wind sweeping down through the tunnel, but Jack's hand still moved automatically to where his sidearm would once have been.

Tara's anti-weapons policy was another example of civilian weakness, one he regretted obeying right now.

"We need to hurry." Jack's tone left no room for debate. "Collect everything in a pile over here, then we can decide what to take. I'll start on that side."

Jack watched Barclay kneel among the bones, his hands moving with exaggerated care as he started to sort through the treasure.

The writer could have his share. Let him run back to his academic circles with whatever story he concocted. None of it would matter when everything fell apart. Civilization's veneer would crack when survival was on the line, no matter how many useless papers and permits and prehistoric bones remained.

But as he watched, Jack noticed Barclay wrapped each artifact in strips of sacking from a stack in the corner. He lingered too long on each piece. He kept looking over at the door, as if preparing to run, and there was a slight sheen of sweat on his forehead despite the chamber's chill. All classic signs of someone fighting their conscience — and losing.

The writer was too quiet, too careful. Men like that could be dangerous. They thought too much, remembered too much, even years later, and Barclay's particular talent for spinning stories into bestsellers made him an especially problematic loose end.

"This is remarkable craftsmanship," Barclay murmured, turning a chalice in his flashlight beam. "The indigenous influence on the decorative elements suggests—"

"Focus," Jack barked. "I'm not here for an art history lesson."

Even as he spoke, his mind was already gaming out alternate scenarios.

The storm provided perfect cover, not just for theft but for potentially cleaning up any complications. The desert had swallowed secrets down here before.

It could do so again.

Jack kept detonation cord and charges back in the storeroom. Old habits from his military days. Always be prepared.

One well-placed charge could bring this whole chamber down, erasing all evidence of their discovery under the guise of storm damage. And if Barclay happened to be investigating the site when it collapsed, well, that would just be an unfortunate consequence of his curiosity.

"Change of plan." Jack kept his voice neutral. "Our DNA

must be on everything down here. We can't leave it to be discovered. It's too much of a liability."

Barclay looked up from where he knelt, his face pale in the harsh beam of the flashlight. "What are you suggesting?"

"A small, controlled demolition with a timer so we can get out unscathed. I used to do similar things in Afghanistan. It will look like a natural collapse from the storm, and will bury all the evidence."

"You can't be serious." Barclay's voice cracked. "This is a priceless historical site. The archaeological significance alone—"

"Is exactly why it needs to disappear." Jack moved closer, looming over the smaller man. "You think they'll let you keep any of this if it's officially discovered? You think the Feds will cut you in for a finder's fee?"

Barclay's grip tightened on the chalice he held, knuckles white against the golden surface.

"I have explosives," Jack continued. "It will be a quick setup and the storm will mask any noise. By morning, this will just be another sealed cave."

"But the bones..." Barclay said weakly.

"Looks like they already had a proper burial." Jack gestured to the carefully arranged remains. "We're just adding a few more layers of dirt."

He turned away, heading for the tunnel back to the storeroom. "I'll get the charges. I won't be long. Start sorting what we're taking tonight. Prioritize anything that can't be traced."

Jack strode back to the storeroom, the sound of the storm getting louder as he returned to the hotel's perimeter. He really should be up there checking on everything, but after Tara's dismissive attitude, that could wait.

His gear cache was exactly where he'd left it, hidden behind a false panel at the other end of the storeroom. There was enough explosive to bring down the chamber but not damage the hotel's foundation. He had done similar work in Afghanistan, collapsing tunnel networks while preserving above-ground structures, and that experience would come in handy tonight.

By the time Jack returned to the crypt, Barclay had arranged many of the artifacts into neat piles. The writer's hands shook slightly as he wrapped another golden cup in a torn cloth, intent on his task.

Jack worked efficiently, placing the explosives at key structural points. The old stone would come down easily, as centuries of seepage had already weakened it. He snaked the detonation cord around the crypt, connecting each charge in a precise pattern.

"We'll recover the items during the second half of the banquet," Jack explained as he worked. "The wine will flow. The band will start, and everyone will be distracted. The storm gives us perfect cover to move things out through the service entrance. I'll have a maintenance truck waiting and we'll head for Vegas."

"And then?" Barclay's voice was barely a whisper.

"We'll fence it all, split the money, and go our separate ways." Jack attached the final detonator, checking the connection. "And never speak of this again."

He turned and held out his hand. It was a beat too long before Barclay shook it, and the writer's palm was cold and damp against his own callused grip.

"Meet me here just after nine," Jack said. "Don't be late." He waved down the tunnel. "Hurry back now, you need to look the part at dinner."

Jack watched Barclay scurry off. Only when the sound of his footsteps had completely faded did Jack allow himself a cold smile.

Let Barclay think they had a deal. Let him dream about his share of the gold. By morning, the only one leaving with anything would be Jack.

As he made his final checks, the detonator warm in his pocket, it seemed as if the skulls watched from their niches, their hollow eyes holding centuries of secrets. Soon, they would have one more to keep.

CHAPTER 13

SIMONE OPENED THE REFRIGERATION unit and selected the blood bag she'd positioned on top of the pile.

She steadied her breathing before carrying it through to the master bedroom where Maxwell lay on the bed, scrolling on his phone.

"Still no service. What kind of place is this if a storm can disrupt the connection? Surely, they have a backup. They promised connectivity at all times."

Simone hung the blood bag on an IV stand and prepared the line. "You could just relax. It would lower your cortisol, and isn't that better for the treatment?"

"You're right." Maxwell put his phone down and rolled up the sleeve of his casual linen shirt. "Dr. Matsuda thinks we could push the improvements further. The key is getting even younger donors in peak physical condition. College athletes are ideal, and they need the money."

Through the suite's open double doors, Simone could hear the faint sounds of Isla laughing at some teen drama she was currently obsessed with. The joyful sound, so innocent and unaware, eased the tightness in Simone's chest.

Just an hour ago, she had stood at the window, watching the wall of sand approach, her heart almost clawing from her throat. She imagined Isla out there, somewhere in the chaos, her small body dashed against the rocks, broken amongst pieces of a dune buggy.

The catastrophic scenarios had nearly broken her perfect composure, and she wanted to scream at Maxwell to do something, send help, use his money and influence to protect their child.

He'd barely looked up from his phone when she expressed her worry, muttering something about the resort's more than adequate safety protocols and how she molly-coddled her daughter too much.

Their daughter, technically, though Maxwell's interest in fatherhood had waned along with his interest in Simone herself. Isla was just another achievement, like his companies or his art collection. Something to display at carefully selected moments, then return to storage out of view.

Simone's fingers tightened on the IV line as fierce love and fiercer protection surged through her.

Isla was the only pure thing to come from this marriage of calculation. She grew up with all the privileges Simone had once dreamed of, but somehow hadn't become spoiled by them. She still said thank you to hotel staff and remained excited about small things like seeing a fox in the desert. She hadn't stopped talking about how kind Casey the guide was out there, and how knowledgeable about desert life. Isla had even been excited by the race back to the hotel in the dune buggy rather than scared by it. The thought of her daughter becoming like other children in their social circle — entitled, obsessed with status, empty — kept Simone awake at night.

The sound of Isla's laughter drifted through once more, and Simone allowed herself a small, genuine smile. *Soon, my love. Soon we'll both be free.*

She bent to Maxwell. "Hold still," she murmured, swabbing the crook of his arm with an alcohol wipe. The sharp medicinal scent mixed with his exclusive cologne, a custom blend that cost more than most homes.

His skin was warm to the touch, still tanned from their recent trip to his private island. Still firm too, but was that a slight looseness beneath? Time was winning, despite all his expensive defenses, but time was also all they had.

Simone's hand trembled on the IV line as memories crashed over her.

Maxwell dancing with a tiny Isla at her fifth birthday party, his face lit with genuine joy as he twirled their giggling daughter.

Long walks on their private beach in the Maldives, when his fingers had intertwined with hers so naturally, before status and science consumed him.

The way he'd held her after her father died, his strength like a fortress against grief.

Even now, under the tweakments and facelift and Botox he insisted on using, Simone could still see traces of the man who had once looked at her with such tenderness, before youth and beauty became commodities to be measured and maintained.

Doubt crept in like the storm's shadows across the floor.

She could still switch the bag for untampered blood, claim it looked faulty, let nature take its course instead of becoming a murderer. The thought of Isla one day discovering the truth made her throat close.

She reached for the blood bag.

Maxwell's hand caught her wrist, his grip still strong. "Nature is the enemy, darling. We have the power to transcend it. To become something more." His eyes were fever-bright with conviction. "The wealthy have a responsibility to push the boundaries. To show what's possible. You could wind the clock back and once again be the woman you were years ago. The woman I was attracted to."

He let her wrist go and trailed a fingertip along her arm, down across her waist and up her thigh under her robe—

Simone deftly twisted away. "You don't want to be late with the treatment. Let me get it started now."

Maxwell's words strengthened her resolve.

The man she'd loved was already gone, replaced by this obsessive stranger who saw his family as just another dataset to be optimized. Her fingers steadied on the line. She hadn't chosen this path lightly, but she would walk it to its end. For Isla. Always for Isla.

Once his money was safely under her control, they would build a different life. In Paris maybe, or one of those towns in Switzerland. Somewhere Isla could attend a European school and make real friends instead of networking connections. Where the weight of her American wealth and status wouldn't distort her future.

They could live simply. Well, as simply as Maxwell's fortune — and her lifestyle — would allow. Isla could learn about art and history and culture by seeing it in person at museums and performances. She could develop into a young woman without the pressure of the expectations of the wealthy crushing her into a predetermined mold.

Simone checked the IV connection to the blood bag one more time and calmed her breathing before turning back to her husband. She slid the needle into his arm with practiced precision, then adjusted the drip rate. It determined exactly how long it would take for the tainted blood to work its way through his system, and she needed the timing to perfectly match the evening ahead.

"I need to get going. The spa is offering a storm special." She gathered her silk robe around her and tightened the tie around her waist. "And you'll want to rest before the banquet. You know how the treatment makes you sleepy."

"Always so practical," Maxwell murmured, his eyes already heavy. "That's why I chose you."

No, Simone thought as she moved toward the door. You chose me because I was young and beautiful and desperate enough to play whatever role you wanted. Now you have Emma for that — but not for long.

As Maxwell closed his eyes, Simone padded softly out of the room. She checked on Isla, who was lost in some game on her iPad, her earlier adventures forgotten.

"I won't be long, darling."

"Mm, see you later."

Simone slipped out of the suite and headed down the hallway, her silk robe whispering against her skin.

The storm penetrated even here, making the windows creak and shudder. Sand whirled against the glass like an angry spirit, casting strange shadows across the hotel's cream-colored walls. The overhead lights flickered briefly before steadying again.

Simone welcomed the storm's violence. It was easier to attribute her trembling hands and elevated breathing to the natural fears of disaster and her daughter's safety rather than what she had set in motion back in the suite.

As she rounded the corner toward the spa, Jack emerged from a side door marked Basement Storage.

Simone stopped short, her heart pounding in her chest as she looked at him. His tactical gear looked out of place against the hotel's carefully cultivated luxury, like a weapon in an art gallery.

"Jack." His name escaped her lips before she could stop it.

He turned, and for a moment, time folded back on itself.

She was twenty-eight, fresh off another failed audition, finding comfort in losing herself in his embrace. His eyes still held the same predatory focus, and now they fixed on her.

Simone walked closer, letting her robe fall open slightly. "It's been a long time."

She touched his arm, feeling the tension in his muscles through the fabric of his shirt. The chemistry was still there, crackling between them like the storm's lightning outside.

"Fifteen years," he said, his voice rough. Something flickered across his features. Remembrance, perhaps, or regret.

The lines around his eyes were deeper now, his face more weathered, but he still carried himself with the military precision that had first drawn her to him.

"Join me in the spa?" She let her voice drop to the husky whisper he used to love. "For old times' sake?"

Jack pulled away sharply, his eyes hardening as his gaze raked over her. "You're not twenty-eight anymore, Simone."

His words were like a slap, precise and devastating. She kept her smile in place, though now it felt brittle enough to shatter.

He turned away. "I have work to do. Enjoy your stay."

Simone watched Jack stride away, his boots silent on the thick carpet, until he disappeared around the corner. Only then did she let her shoulders slump, allowing the mask to slip for just a moment. Then she pulled herself up and straightened her spine. Who the hell did he think he was?

At the spa, the glass doors whispered open at Simone's approach, releasing a wave of eucalyptus-scented air. Inside, the lighting was artfully dimmed, and the sound of the storm was muted to a distant roar.

"Mrs. Carver-Scott." The spa manager was all professional solicitude and soft tones. "Your massage therapist is ready."

Simone followed her to a private treatment room with the soft sound of running water and the sweet smell of jasmine in the air. She lay face-down on the table and let skilled hands work the tension from her shoulders.

As she lost herself in sensation, Simone considered a new angle for what lay ahead.

Jack's presence complicated things, but he might also be exactly what she needed. There had been something in his eyes when he emerged from that basement door. Guilt, perhaps. Definitely a secret of some kind, something she could exploit.

If questions were asked about Maxwell's death, who

better to implicate than the ex-military security chief with a dubious interest in the apocalypse?

Jack had always attracted trouble, drawn to risky situations and shady choices. Back when they were together, there had always been side deals, questionable contacts, plans within plans. If the police investigated him, they would no doubt find plenty of evidence of illegal activity.

Simone let out a small gasp as the massage therapist found a knot in her shoulder. The woman murmured an apology, but Simone welcomed the discomfort. It helped her focus.

She could almost see it playing out. The grieving widow, shocked to discover that the head of security had long harbored a grudge against her wealthy husband. Perhaps he'd even tried to blackmail Maxwell and threatened to expose something about the source of his anti-aging treatments.

In the chaos of the storm, anything could happen.

Simone smiled into the cradle of the massage table, letting the tension drain from her body as the therapist's hands worked their magic.

Soon, she would be free, and if Jack had to take the fall, well, he should have remembered she'd always been a better actor than he gave her credit for.

CHAPTER 14

RAFAEL STALKED THE PERIMETER of his luxury suite, his custom-made hunting rifle dead weight in his hands. It was useless here in this climate-controlled cage of marble and glass.

Outside, the sandstorm painted apocalyptic scenes in shades of red-brown and ochre. The wind's howl stirred something primal in his blood, reminding him of the jaguar's roar he'd recorded in Brazil, just before—

He pushed the memory away. That controversy had nearly ended his career, but the views — oh, the millions of views and new followers — had certainly been worth it.

"Mierda!" The curse echoed off the suite's high ceilings as he checked his phone again.

Almost twenty million followers waiting for their daily dose of outrage and spectacle, and all he had to show them was a damn rabbit. He couldn't even post that since the internet was down.

His video thumbnails usually featured exotic prey, endangered species, and apex predators. The death of such creatures made conservationists weep and his fans cheer. He couldn't post about the cottontail. He'd be a laughing stock.

Rafael set the rifle down on the king-sized bed as he paced up and down.

The suite's temperature was perfect, the lighting artfully designed, every detail crafted for luxury. But it suffocated him.

He craved the rush of the hunt, the feeling of a creature's life ebbing away as he wielded the knife. He needed blood on his hands.

All for the fans, of course.

His reflection caught his eye in the bedroom's full-length mirror. The red bandana, his trademark look, was instantly recognizable all over the world, but right now, it looked too clean. His fans expected to see it stained with sweat and flecked with gore. They wanted him wrist-deep in some exotic creature's entrails while delivering his signature catchphrase: "This is real food, amigos. No supermarket bullshit here."

Rafael pulled up his latest analytics, stored in the app even offline. The numbers were clear. Engagement dropped sharply without regular content, and the algorithm was merciless. Miss a few days, and you might never recover the momentum.

"Two hundred thousand new followers after the Komodo dragon video," he muttered. "Not bad."

The footage had been incredible. He'd wrestled the giant lizard, his knife glinting in the Indonesian sun, the perfect mix of danger and dominance that his audience craved.

Of course, it had been an old creature, bought from a local zoo and barely a challenge, but Rafael made it look like an epic battle to the death.

After the video, animal rights organizations had called for his arrest — and his sponsored deals had tripled. With the rise of populist politics and the imminent death of woke, even more companies wanted to attach their brand to his carefully cultivated image of primal masculinity and the unapologetic male dominance that had become his trade-mark.

But he had to keep feeding the algorithm — and that was the most challenging beast of all.

He couldn't waste his time sitting out the storm. There must be something he could kill.

Rafael picked up the hotel phone and punched in the numbers for security. Each ring stretched out as his pulse quickened with desperate hope.

"Security," Jack answered in a clipped tone.

Rafael used his camera voice, the one that charmed millions every week. "Jack, mi amigo! Listen, about that hunting expedition we discussed—"

"The storm makes that impossible." The response was flat, final.

"Sure, sure, but you know I can pay extra, right? Maybe you have another option. I heard rumors from the staff about some interesting specimens you might have here?"

A beat of silence.

Rafael held his breath, already imagining the footage. Something exotic, dangerous, deadly. His fans would eat it up.

"Meet me in the interior desert garden," Jack said finally. "Thirty minutes. I need to prep them first."

The line went dead, but Rafael was already moving, gathering his gear with practiced efficiency.

His hands shook slightly as he checked his camera equipment, the memory of his last viral hit playing in his mind. The outrage, the acclaim, the rush of power that came from pushing boundaries, from demonstrating his dominance over nature itself.

Time to do it all over again.

Rafael turned to the mirror and adjusted his bandana until he achieved that perfectly rugged but camera-ready look his brand demanded.

Damn, he was hot. No wonder he had just as many women in his audience as men. Perhaps he could find a fan or two in the staff quarters here after the banquet later. Get some exercise along with his pleasure.

"Time to give them all what they want," Rafael told his reflection, baring his teeth in what his fans called his 'predator smile.'

The suite suddenly felt too small, too tame. He needed violence. He needed to remind everyone that he wasn't just some social media chef. He was an apex predator, a force of nature. Unstoppable.

Rafael checked his hunting knife, tested its keen edge against his thumb.

Let the eco-warriors cry. Let the activists threaten. Every voice raised against him just added more zeros to his bank account and fed the algorithm that made him a star.

"Show time, amigos." He shouldered his camera bag and headed out of the suite.

Rafael's boots echoed along the corridor leading to the interior desert garden. Each step took him deeper into the hotel's artificial wilderness, condensed and curated behind climate-controlled glass walls.

Joshua trees towered overhead, their branches reaching toward the glass ceiling beyond which the storm still raged. Cholla and barrel cacti clustered in artfully arranged groups, their spines gleaming like tiny knives in the filtered light.

The air was carefully maintained at optimal humidity, warm but not scorching. It was nature tamed and packaged for the guests' viewing pleasure. Too sanitized and too safe for Rafael's usual brand of fun, but it was a decent backdrop for what he hoped would be a good show — and whatever it was would be better than a damn rabbit.

He paused in front of a glass-paneled enclosure.

A western diamondback rattlesnake lay coiled, nearly invisible, against the decorative rocks of its enclosure. Its tongue flicked out, tasting his presence, and he admired its deadly elegance. This was genuine nature, not the potted succulents and carefully arranged desert marigolds that dotted the walkway.

"Beautiful, aren't they?" Jack's voice came from the shadows near the service entrance. The head of security moved with a distinctive military grace Rafael recognized as violence held in check. He respected that in a man.

Jack wheeled a large cooler, unmarked and industrial-grade, along the path. "These are even better."

Rafael's pulse quickened. "Show me."

Jack opened the cooler with deliberate slowness. Inside, six clear bags with air holes contained scaled coils of muscle and venom.

Desert horned vipers.

Their scales gleamed like oil-slicked obsidian, their horned heads rising to test the confines of their temporary cells.

"Magnífica," Rafael breathed, already framing shots in his mind.

The dramatic reveal as he reached into the writhing mass. The close-up on the snake's eyes, vertical pupils contracting in the light. The moment of the kill, as his blade severed that elegant head from its body. His viewers would lose their minds.

"Six thousand. Each." Jack's tone was businesslike. "Plus, another five for my discretion."

"Of course." Rafael barely heard the price. He was calculating views, engagement metrics, sponsor opportunities. A video like this could easily clear seven figures in revenue. And the publicity from serving the meat at tonight's banquet? Priceless.

"The venom sacs are intact?"

"Naturally." Jack closed the lid of the cooler. "These aren't pets, they're weapons. One bite contains enough neurotoxin to kill."

Perfect. Rafael could already hear his narration: "Today, amigos, we're going to taste death itself."

He reached for his camera bag. "I'll need help with filming. The angles have to be just right, and I can't have my crew involved since this is not — strictly — legal."

"I can't." Jack stepped away, checking his tactical watch. "I've already been gone too long and I need to do a security sweep before the banquet. The storm's got everyone on edge." He raised an eyebrow. "Surely you can handle a few snakes by yourself?"

Rafael bristled at Jack's tone, and his hand dropped to the knife at his belt, fingers curling around the familiar grip. "No problem, amigo. I work better alone anyway."

Jack tracked the movement, and a smile played around his lips. "Just keep them contained. I don't want to explain any accidents to the owner."

Rafael barely noticed the security chief leave as he set up his first shot, positioning the cooler next to an exhibit of large flat stones shaped by desert winds. The light would catch the reflection of the snakes' scales as he pulled them out.

He moved with practiced efficiency, checking angles and lighting, practicing the scene in his mind as he prepared his camera and his phone setup for different angles.

It was good to do this alone, without his crew. Just like the early days when he ran the entire operation himself. Simple. Streamlined. Perhaps he needed to return to that elemental process and the purity of his own creative vision.

The desert garden provided a perfect stage, all sleek glass and carefully curated wilderness. Through the transparent walls, the sandstorm created an apocalyptic backdrop that made his pulse quicken with creative possibility. Nature's fury versus man's dominance. Raw survival against manufactured safety. His viewers would eat this up.

"Perfect lighting, mi amor," he murmured to his top-of-the-line camera.

He opened the cooler to check on the vipers. They writhed

in the temporary container. Such beautiful creatures. Their hornlike protrusions gave them an almost mythical appearance, perfect for thumbnails. He'd position the most aggressive one front and center when he transferred them.

But he needed them out of those bags first.

Quickly he slit the individual bags that held them so they writhed out, and then emptied the snakes from the cooler into a glass terrarium set up on one of the rocks, the camera capturing their fluid movement.

The space was cramped for six adult vipers, making them more agitated.

Exactly what he wanted.

Angry snakes made for better footage, and he knew how to handle them. The sight of writhing, venomous serpents would evoke primal fear in his viewers, their unease translating to higher engagement.

People wouldn't be able to look away, their horror compelling them to share the video. Fear was a currency in this business.

"Look at you, mis bellezas peligrosas," he crooned, tapping the glass to rile them further. Their heads snapped toward the vibration, forked tongues testing the air. "You're going to make me famous… Well, more famous."

Lightning flashed through the storm-dark sky, illuminating the swirling sand that battered against the glass. The dramatic lighting sent the snakes' shadows dancing across the garden.

Damn, this would be a good video.

Rafael positioned his hunting knife on the flat stone, its Damascus steel blade catching the light. The handle was inlaid with ivory. Illegal in some places, but his followers loved these little details.

Next to it, he arranged his snake-handling tongs, and a small butane torch for searing the meat.

Perhaps he could even use the flame on one of the snakes

while it still lived. That would amplify the outrage even more.

He grinned as he readied himself to start the recording.

The door to the garden suddenly swung open with a soft hydraulic hiss.

Rafael's fingers tightened on his camera grip as the fashion influencer, Grace Lin, walked inside. She'd clearly come to film her own content, but thankfully he'd got here first.

Her eyes widened as she saw the snakes — and his knife.

Rafael's grin widened even further. This could be a chance for content gold. His viewers loved conflict, especially with beautiful, privileged women who didn't understand the raw reality of nature.

He quickly hit record on both devices, already scripting the confrontation in his head.

CHAPTER 15

CASEY CHECKED THE DUNE buggies in the adventure garage once again and verified that all the emergency gear was ready — just in case. It calmed her to know that at least something was in her control as the storm raged outside.

The huge garage door rattled behind her in the intensifying wind, threatening to tear free of its moorings. If it somehow came loose, and the storm got inside, all this expensive equipment would be at risk. Casey began to secure what she could.

The first dune buggy was already locked down, its cherry-red chassis gleaming under the fluorescent lights. But the black beast they used for the more adventurous guests kept fighting her efforts.

Casey remembered how Isla's face lit up when she saw it earlier that day. Something about the girl tugged at Casey's heart — Isla had a wild curiosity that reminded her of herself at that age. The restrictive boundaries of privilege made it even more necessary for the girl to break free and taste real adventure.

The weight of expectation clearly wrapped around Isla like invisible chains already. Her mother's concern about appearances, her father's pointed comments about suitable activities for a Carver-Scott.

A very different chain had enveloped Casey back in her small Somerset town, where everyone knew everyone else's business, and where her tarnished reputation followed her like a shadow.

A fresh gust of wind howled through the gaps around the garage door, carrying with it a spray of sand that tasted of metal and salt.

Casey pulled her bandana higher over her nose, but the fine particles still found their way into her mouth, her eyes, underneath her collar.

The cable finally caught, and Casey yanked it tight, securing it with a quick-release lock just in case the buggy was needed.

Her shoulders ached from wrestling with the equipment, but she couldn't rest yet. The vehicles were their only reliable means of evacuation if things went wrong — and in her experience, things could go catastrophically wrong with frightening speed. It was important to be prepared. As much as she couldn't stand Jack, that belief was something they had in common.

A sound cut through the roar of the wind outside. High-pitched, mechanical.

An alarm.

Casey tilted her head and listened hard. The wind distorted the sound, but after a moment, she pinpointed its likely source.

The water treatment facility.

Maintenance would be busy with the storm damage, so she'd check it on the way back.

Casey zipped her jacket up to her chin and pressed the garage's heavy door shut behind her, checking twice to ensure it was properly latched.

As she stepped out from behind the building's shelter, the full force of the wind hit her like a physical blow. Sand pelted her exposed skin, each grain a tiny bullet that stung and burned. She squinted against the assault, each step a battle as the wind tried to knock her off balance.

The water treatment facility was only a hundred yards away, but distance meant little in a sandstorm. The sky had darkened to a deep ochre, and visibility dropped by the minute. The resort's main building was now just a hulking shadow blurred by curtains of shifting sand.

The facility's door, sealed shut by the pressure differential, fought Casey like a living thing. She threw her full weight against it until it finally gave and she stumbled inside.

Something was wrong.

The familiar hum of machinery had changed, becoming jarring, stuttering. And the smell — her stomach lurched as a wave of chemical stench hit her.

Casey walked over to the main treatment tank. It should have held crystal-clear water but now churned with dark sludge that roiled and bubbled, releasing fumes that made her eyes water.

She hurried to the control panel.

Red warning lights flashed across the displays. The pH readings were off the charts, and the viscosity sensors screamed urgent warnings. The contamination was spreading throughout the entire system of the hotel complex.

The resort had emergency water reserves, but the demands of these exclusive guests could swiftly deplete them. Cut off by the storm, without access to water, they could be facing potential disaster.

Casey backed away from the controls, running one hand through her sand-caked hair. She needed to report this now.

Jack crossed her mind. The head of security would be the logical person to tell. But his smirk and the way he sneered at her suggestions about improving emergency protocols held her back. Tourist-coddling, he called it, in that tone that set her teeth on edge. He didn't take her seriously enough to heed her warning, and the bastard probably had his own secret water cache somewhere, along with enough ammunition to supply a small army.

Tara certainly needed to know. The hotel's owner might be demanding and occasionally erratic, but she understood that their guests' safety came first. She would hate a PR disaster, perhaps even more than a technical one.

Casey headed back through maintenance and up into the main hotel building. She rounded the corner to Tara's office at full speed, nearly colliding with an expensive pottery display of desert succulents.

The office door stood open, but Tara was nowhere to be seen.

Casey stood at the threshold, years of ingrained professional boundaries warring with the urgency of the situation.

"Tara?" she called out. "Hello?"

Casey hesitated in the doorway, her own unpaid wages weighing heavily on her mind, as well as what she'd heard from other local workers. A month's worth of apologetic emails and vague promises about temporary cash flow issues.

The water crisis couldn't wait, but neither could she ignore this chance to see what else was going on. After the tragedy in the cave, Casey promised herself never to ignore warning signs again. And lately, the signs at the Desert Sanctuary had been flashing red.

She stepped inside, heart hammering against her ribs at the trespass, and circled the desk, noticing a stack of invoices piled up in an in-tray. The top one had Final Notice stamped across it, with a sum that made her throat go dry. Six figures, just for water treatment supplies.

She shuffled the papers to find another for staff insurance premiums marked Urgent: Policy Cancellation Warning.

"What the hell?" Casey whispered, checking more in the pile. The amounts were staggering. Maintenance contracts, food suppliers, utilities. Each page told the same story. The hotel was hemorrhaging money and Tara clearly needed cash, and soon.

A sudden gust of wind rattled the windows, making Casey jump. The storm's eerie light filtered through the blinds, casting shadows across the desk as her mind raced with the implications.

The sound of footsteps registered too late.

"What are you doing in here?"

Casey spun around, an invoice crumpling in her too-tight grip.

Tara stood in the doorway, backlit by the corridor's emergency lights. The storm had frayed Tara's usually perfect appearance. Her designer dress was dusted with sand, her carefully styled hair beginning to frizz in the rising humidity. But it was her eyes that stopped Casey cold. They held the same desperation she'd seen in trapped animals, the kind that would chew off their own limb to escape.

"I—" Casey's mouth was desert-dry. "The water treatment facility—"

Tara crossed the space in three quick strides, snatching the invoice from Casey's hand. "These are none of your concern. Everything is under control."

Up close, she could see the cracks in Tara's perfect facade. The slight yellowing of her eyes, the foundation caked over dark circles, the way she swayed almost imperceptibly, as if the ground beneath them wasn't quite stable.

"The water system is contaminated," Casey pushed on, even as every instinct screamed at her to retreat. "It's spreading. If we don't stop it—"

"I said everything is under control." Tara's voice dropped lower, taking on a dangerous edge. "Focus on your job, Casey. That's all you need to worry about." Her lips curved in what might have been meant as a smile, but looked more like a grimace. "Or do you want that caving accident to become common knowledge? You'll never work in the adventure industry again if I amplify your part in it."

The threat hung in the air.

Casey took a step toward the door, then another, her hands raised in surrender. "Okay, I'm going."

"The banquet starts in an hour." Tara's tone shifted to something artificially bright. "Make sure you're presentable. I'm relying on you and the other staff to keep the guests entertained while the storm is still with us."

Tara turned to her desk. A clear dismissal.

Casey retreated and pulled the office door shut behind her, the quiet click of the latch like a full stop on her illusions about the Sanctuary.

She would tell the head of maintenance about the water treatment plant and hope they could get it under control, but something deeper was wrong here. The contamination was just a symptom of a larger disease eating away at the foundations of the hotel.

As she walked back through the corridors, Casey imagined dark tendrils of pollution spreading beneath her feet like black veins through the desert's flesh. The same way Tara's desperation had leaked through her perfect mask, the way Jack's violence simmered beneath his professional surface, the way every guest carried their own poison behind wealthy facades.

Casey touched the wall as she walked, feeling the building's subtle vibration through her fingertips under the power of the storm's assault.

The Desert Sanctuary's heartbeat was arrhythmic now, its systems failing one by one like organs shutting down.

Soon the poison would reach every corner, just as the storm's violence would find every weakness. And they were all trapped here, breathing the same contaminated air, drinking the same tainted water, while the desert waited patient and eternal beyond the failing walls.

Casey shook away her darker thoughts and took a deep breath. She would dress for the banquet and play her part in this charade. One more night and the storm would pass and all would be well. It had to be.

CHAPTER 16

Rafael grinned as Grace Lin stalked toward him, her expression contorted with rage.

"Welcome to the show, princesa," he called out, letting his accent thicken in the way his fans expected.

The camera would love the contrast between them. Her designer dress versus his deliberately rugged appearance. Her femininity contrasted with his ultra-masculine predatory nature.

"Want to help me prepare some authentic desert cuisine?"

The snakes writhed in the terrarium, agitated by the voices and movement. Their scales made a dry, whispering sound against the glass that raised the hair on Rafael's arms. Fear was good. Fear got views. Fear made people feel alive.

He adjusted his bandana, squared his shoulders, and gave the camera his signature predator's smile. He knew what his audience wanted. Not just death, but the dance leading up to it.

Drama. Conflict. The raw demonstration of man's dominance over nature.

The storm intensified beyond the glass walls, as if nature itself wanted to join the fun.

"Shall we begin?" he asked his invisible audience, reaching for the snake tongs. Two of the vipers raised their horned heads, tracking his movement as their tongues flicked through the air.

Grace strode toward him as fast as she could in her towering heels. "You monster!"

Rafael's camera caught every detail. The way her carefully curated calm shattered into genuine outrage, the tremor in her manicured hands as she pointed accusingly at the terrarium.

Perfect. Raw emotion always increased engagement.

"Those snakes are protected!" Grace's voice cracked with genuine anger. Not the manufactured kind Rafael usually saw from influencers. "They're a vital part of Death Valley's ecosystem!"

Rafael knew the camera angle would capture both her righteous anger and the writhing snakes behind them. The creatures were not even from the local area, which would make her privileged moral outrage even more dramatic.

"Do you have any idea how many desert species are already endangered?" She was building to a crescendo now, her voice carrying the polished tones of expensive schools and the lingo of environmental activism conferences. "And here you are, treating them like props for your disgusting spectacle!"

Rafael kept his predator's smile in place as she spat the words, letting her rage wash over him.

Each accusation was another potential clip, another shareable moment. His followers would dissect this interaction for weeks, taking sides, starting fights in his comments section. The algorithm loved controversy.

"Such passion, princesa," he drawled when she finally paused for breath. "But tell me, have you ever killed your own meat? Ever felt the life drain from a living creature, felt its last breath against your skin before eating its flesh?"

Rafael reached into the terrarium, his movements deliberate and smooth as one of the vipers tracked his approach, its scales gleaming like wet ink.

With practiced skill, Rafael grasped it behind the head with the tongs, lifting it from its glass prison.

"This beauty" — he addressed the camera directly now, holding the writhing serpent aloft — "is a desert horned viper. One of nature's perfect killers. Its venom can stop a man's heart in minutes." The snake twisted in his grip, muscles rippling beneath its scales. "Life feeds on death. Strength devours weakness."

Grace looked pale, but she stood her ground. She was brave. He had to give her that. Most influencers would have run by now.

Rafael's free hand found his knife, the Damascus steel reflecting the storm's light in its intricate patterns. His blade had tasted the blood of countless rare species and now would add another to the list.

"Our ancestors lived by these truths, and we must fight to rediscover them in this sanitized world."

The snake's writhing grew frantic. Rafael could feel its strength, its ancient killing power.

But he was stronger. He was the apex predator here.

With a single motion, he slammed the viper down onto the stone slab and sliced the blade lightning fast, severing flesh and bone with surgical precision.

Blood spurted from the writhing body, so much brighter than mammal blood, almost luminous in the storm light.

Rafael leaned in close, letting the camera capture every detail as he caught drops of spurting blood in his mouth.

The taste was electric. Copper and salt and something older, something that sparked inside the primitive parts of his brain.

His fans would go wild when they saw this, sharing screenshots, creating memes. The more outrage, the further the algorithm would spread it.

"You're insane," Grace choked out, staggering back, her hand over her mouth. Even in horror, she instinctively found the best angle for the camera. "You won't get away with this. I have millions of followers. When they see—"

"When they see," Rafael cut her off, blood staining his lips, "they'll share. They'll engage." He smiled, knowing how he must look. The primitive warrior, the untamed beast in their civilized garden. "That's what we do, no? We give them spectacle. We give them something to rage about in their comfortable homes. The only difference, princesa, is that I don't pretend to be anything other than what I am."

Grace stumbled toward the door. "I'll make sure everyone knows about this. Every animal rights group, every conservation activist. I'll burn your brand to the ground."

Rafael laughed as she fled. There was no such thing as bad publicity, and Grace knew that. Every outraged comment, every call for his cancellation, even the death threats. All fed the beast the algorithm, driving the value of his brand higher as the dollars rolled in.

Alone once more, he turned back to the remaining snakes, their scales shimmering in the apocalyptic light. Five more videos to film, five more chances to give his fans what they craved, and he would edit them into one glorious montage.

As blood pulsed from the snake's body, lightning split the sky, so bright it left purple afterimages dancing in his vision. Thunder crashed immediately after, the sound amplified by the garden's glass walls.

The massive windows flexed, creating distortions in the apocalyptic landscape beyond. The artificial lighting flickered overhead.

"Perfecto," Rafael murmured, adjusting his camera to capture the dramatic atmosphere from a different angle. "Time for a real show."

As he turned to the terrarium, the largest viper — the one he'd marked for his grand finale — darted for the rim of its enclosure.

Its muscular body swiftly slid up and over its companions with fluid grace, scales rasping like a whispered warning. It reached the top edge of the glass, exploiting the cramped space to push itself higher on the bodies of its kin.

Rafael lunged for it with the tongs but couldn't get a grip.

"Mierda!" he cursed as the viper dropped to the floor.

It slithered toward him, recognizing the threat in its path.

Rafael's heart lurched, his professional confidence giving way to primal fear. This wasn't part of the show. This wasn't controlled chaos for the camera.

He grabbed for his knife, the blade suddenly awkward in his sweat-slicked hand.

The snake was fast — so much faster than he'd expected — moving like a liquid shadow across the artificial desert landscape.

Rafael tried to dart away, but time slowed as the viper reared and struck.

Its fangs sank into his skin just above his designer hiking boots, punching through his desert-style chinos into vulnerable flesh.

The pain was sharp, followed by a spreading warmth.

"No, no, no…" Rafael stumbled backward, reaching for the support of the stone, his camera forgotten.

His arm caught the terrarium with the remaining snakes inside, knocking it sideways and off the stone.

The crash of breaking glass.

The remaining snakes slithered out of the wreckage onto the floor, their scales catching the storm's lightning as their primitive brains registered only threat.

Rafael could only moan as two more struck him, each bite a white-hot needle, injecting liquid fire into his veins.

The knife clattered from fingers that were already beginning to tingle and go numb.

"Help," he tried to call out, but his throat had tightened so much he could only gasp.

His legs gave way, and he crashed to the glass-strewn floor.

Rafael reached for his phone, his vision already beginning to blur as he pushed over the tripod and crawled to his fallen device. The screen swam before him, the emergency contact numbers dancing away from his unresponsive fingers even as he saw there was still no signal.

His body convulsed as the venom worked through his system with brutal efficiency, each heartbeat spreading the poison further. His muscles seized and spasmed. He could feel his throat closing, his lungs struggling for air.

Beside him, the fallen phone continued to record. His last coherent thought was of the viewing numbers this would generate. His death might be his most viral content ever.

Lightning strobed through the garden, painting everything in flashes of purple-white brilliance. Each flash showed Rafael's body in a different agonized pose, twisting, convulsing, and slowly stilling as the venom did its work.

His eyes remained open, glazed and unseeing, his body succumbing to the savagery that had fueled his brand, as the snakes slithered away from his corpse into the carefully maintained vegetation of the desert garden.

CHAPTER 17

THE GRAND DINING ROOM hung suspended between earth and storm, a bubble of civilization floating above Death Valley's savage beauty. When the architects had designed this raised level within the dome, Tara had wanted it to almost float, like the clouds across the vast sky. Now she stood at the threshold, allowing herself a moment to savor the perfection of what she had created — and what she desperately needed to preserve.

The expanse glowed with the warm light of hand-forged copper lamps, their delicate filaments casting patterns across the walls mimicking the constellations visible on clear nights. Each table channeled the beauty of understated wealth, with hand-blown glasses in colors drawn from the desert, amber like the morning light on Zabriskie Point, deep rose from the mineral-stained cliffs, and pale gold as the salt flats at dawn.

Above it all, the vast glass dome that had nearly bankrupted her stretched toward the storm-dark sky. It brought nature into the hotel and so far, it had been worth every cent.

Lightning flickered through the darkness above, drawing gasps of appreciation from the guests. The sound made Tara's throat tighten. They saw beauty where she now saw threat, entertainment where she counted structural stress points and load-bearing tolerances.

Her fingers worried at the silk of her designer dress, a nervous tell she quickly suppressed. The fabric had been specially dyed to match the rose shade on the tables, so she was almost an extension of the hotel itself. Every detail mattered tonight. Every element had to reinforce the illusion of perfect control over the savage landscape outside.

The storm battered against the glass above with increasing intensity, but the guests smiled and lifted their phones to capture nature's drama, their faces lit by brief flashes of lightning, even as the howl of the wind penetrated the thick glass.

'The desert gives, and the desert takes,' her father's voice whispered. 'Every debt must be paid in full.'

How many debts had Tara accumulated in building this place? Not just the financial ones that kept her awake at night, but the deeper ones — to her heritage and to the land itself?

Tara pushed the thought away. The debts could wait.

She focused instead on her staff's choreographed movements. They were doing well despite the fact that so many were missing due to the storm. Servers glided between tables with practiced grace, offering perfectly paired wines and delicate canapés infused with the essence of desert plants. Their uniforms echoed the natural color palette, making them almost emerge from and dissolve back into the sandstone walls like spirits.

A violent gust made the dome shudder, the sound carrying even over the carefully modulated background music.

Tara held her breath, counting seconds until the vibration settled.

The engineers had assured her the structure could withstand a hundred-year storm event, but those same reports had come with price tags that forced her to cut corners.

Maxwell Carver-Scott's distinctive voice carried across the room, drawing her attention as the tech billionaire guided his wife and daughter toward their prime table nearest the windows. His potential investment could transform Tara's struggles into success and ensure a bright future for the Sanctuary. Perhaps more Sanctuary signature hotels in other deserts around the world. There were so many options.

She took a step toward the family, then frowned.

There was something wrong with Maxwell's movements, a slight unsteadiness, and a sheen of sweat glinted on his forehead despite the carefully controlled temperature.

Lightning split the sky once more, painting the space in stark purple-white relief.

The glass dome caught and amplified the flash, creating a moment where every glass, every piece of polished silver, and every facet of Tara's carefully constructed world blazed with cold fire.

In that frozen instant, she saw a vision of her guests transformed, their designer clothes and perfect manners stripped away, revealing the primitive creatures that lurked beneath civilization's thin veneer.

Then darkness rushed back in, and with it the familiar weight of her role. Tara drew herself up, shoulders straight, chin lifted to the perfect angle. The mask settled into place with practiced ease. The capable owner, the perfect hostess, the woman who tamed the desert itself to create a sanctuary of luxury.

Tara stepped forward into the warm light, gliding between the elegantly set tables and groups of guests. She gave a welcoming smile here, a touch on the arm there, readjusting things as she went, conducting the orchestra of the evening with effortless grace.

A deep roll of thunder shook the dome, making the glasses shudder on the tables.

Several guests glanced up nervously, but Tara merely laughed, conveying both amusement and absolute confidence.

"Nature's percussion section. The acoustics in here are remarkable during a storm. Just wait until you hear the wind harmonics later. It's like having front row seats at the symphony."

Grace Lin, the influencer-turned-activist, shot her a skeptical look from where she sat rigid in her chair. "As long as the glass holds." Her voice dripped with barely concealed disdain. "Though I suppose sustainability doesn't extend to protecting the wildlife, does it? Did you know your celebrity chef is in the garden right now, slaughtering protected species for clicks and likes?"

Tara's carefully maintained smile didn't waver, though her temples throbbed with stress. These influencers were becoming more trouble than they were worth. All that reach and engagement meant nothing if they turned their followers' rage against the resort, and Grace had millions of them, all passionate about environmental causes.

"The dome was built with advanced engineering technology," Tara assured her, deliberately sidestepping the accusation about Rafael. "The glass flexes with pressure. It's a fascinating process. I'd love to tell you about the sustainable materials we used."

But Grace wouldn't be deflected. "He's killing snakes. Desert horned vipers. I saw them myself." Her voice rose slightly, drawing unwanted attention from nearby tables. "They're a vital part of the ecosystem. You can't just—"

"I'll have someone look into it immediately," Tara cut her off smoothly, catching the eye of one of her reliable waitstaff.

She gestured him over with an elegant flick of her wrist. "Please find Mr. Ortiz and remind him that all activities must align with our sustainability policies."

As the waiter hurried away, Tara suppressed a flash of irritation.

Rafael was meant to provide a dramatic centerpiece for tonight's dinner, something spectacular to distract the guests from the growing crisis. She'd specifically instructed him to keep his more controversial activities away from the main resort areas, but the man had no subtlety, no understanding of their clientele's delicate sensibilities. They wanted the illusion of wilderness, not its bloody reality.

Thankfully, she'd insisted Jean-Luc, her head chef, prepare a backup plan. The local-ingredient tasting menu was less theatrical than Rafael's promised spectacle, but it would satisfy even the most discriminating palates. The guests would never know they were getting the understudy performance instead of the star.

"I assure you," Tara told Grace, letting an edge of steel enter her voice, "we take our environmental responsibilities seriously."

She'd learned long ago that conviction mattered more than truth.

Tara moved on before Grace could ask for specifics and continued to circulate amongst the guests — a compliment here, a touch there.

But even as Tara performed her rounds, Casey's questions from earlier clawed at the edge of her thoughts. The British adventure guide had seen too much in the office, but she also had her own secrets, her own desperate reasons for being here in Death Valley. Would that be enough to keep her quiet?

The storm suddenly intensified, sand thudding against the glass like thousands of fists demanding entry.

Simone Carver-Scott flinched at the violent sound, while her daughter Isla pressed closer to the windows, her eyes wide with fascination.

The contrast between mother and child struck Tara as telling. One caged by luxury, the other still capable of genuine wonder. Something in Isla's fearless curiosity reminded Tara of herself as a child, before she'd learned to hide her true nature behind perfectly applied lipstick and carefully curated designer labels.

She approached a table of older women, supposedly an artists' collective from Santa Fe, though their immaculate manicures and designer resort wear suggested more dabbling than dedication. They were the Sanctuary's perfect target demographic. Wealthy enough to afford the price, hungry enough for authenticity to pay even more for a genuine desert experience.

"I've always thought storms strip away our artificial barriers," Tara said, letting a hint of her grandmother's rhythmic cadence enter her voice. It was a calculated risk. Too much 'native wisdom' might make these women uncomfortable, but just enough made them feel special. Initiated. "They remind us of our essential connection to the natural world."

The words flowed smooth as honey, practiced until they sounded authentic. Yet underneath, she felt the familiar twist of shame. Her grandmother would be appalled to see her commodifying their traditions this way, turning sacred knowledge into sound bites for wealthy tourists.

But her grandmother hadn't faced bank loans and contractor bills; she hadn't built something from nothing in a world that expected a Native girl to remain invisible and leave ambition to others.

"We're offering a special meditation session tomorrow morning when the storm has passed. It will be a chance to truly ground ourselves in this ancient landscape."

Assuming the meditation instructor could get here. Assuming they still had power tomorrow. Assuming the water system... Tara forced the thoughts away, her smile never faltering.

"My Timbisha ancestors understood storms as messages from the spirit world," she continued, noting how the women leaned forward, eyes bright with the prospect of receiving authentic indigenous wisdom. She rarely claimed her heritage so directly, but desperate times called for desperate measures.

The women practically vibrated with attention now, their fingers twitching as if longing to post about their encounter with a real Native American. Tara's stomach churned with a mixture of disgust and pragmatism. Let them exoticize her if it meant their money kept the Sanctuary alive.

"They are a reminder of nature's power, yes, but also of our responsibility to live in harmony with the desert."

The oldest of the women, wearing enough turquoise jewelry to stock a gift shop, reached out to touch Tara's arm. "You must feel so connected to this land," she breathed.

Tara nodded, hiding the truth behind a practiced smile.

Once, she had felt that connection, back when she'd run wild through these canyons with her cousins, before scholarships and ambition pulled her into another world. Now the desert felt more like a business partner than a relative. One she might have betrayed too many times.

But she'd done it all for a reason. Every compromise, every careful performance, every strategic decision had been in service of proving that a Timbisha woman could build something lasting, something remarkable. Even if it meant burying parts of herself as deep as the foundations of her hotel.

Lightning flashed again, and in the stark illumination, Tara saw Casey watching her from near the service entrance, the guide's expression too knowing, too full of questions that couldn't be answered without bringing everything crashing down.

Thunder followed immediately, and as conversations paused, Tara seized the moment of uncertainty, projecting her voice with calm authority.

"The desert storms remind us of transformation," she said, watching her guests' faces relax as she provided context for their unease. "The landscape appears harsh and unforgiving, but these dramatic moments create incredible beauty. Flash floods sculpt hidden canyons, the wind reveals ancient petroglyphs, and rain awakens dormant seeds that bloom into wildflowers. Perhaps we too can lean into transformation in this time away from our daily routines?"

The group of artist women smiled, some gazing out into the storm with soul-searching eyes. Tara took another breath. She had bought herself a little more time and if she could just get through tonight, the dawn would bring new hope. She was sure of it.

CHAPTER 18

UP IN HIS ROOM, Barclay's hands shook as he poured another miniature of whiskey into a crystal tumbler, trying to calm his thoughts. The mission treasure could bring him enough money to solve all his problems — and following Jack's plan violated every code of archaeology.

He downed the whiskey in one burning gulp, remembering the weight of the Spanish gold coin in his palm, the way it had caught the beam of his flashlight. He thought of Jack and the way the security chief had looked at him, as if weighing up darker options.

Barclay's academic training warred with his baser instincts as he fumbled to straighten his tie. The remains deserved proper excavation, and there could be invaluable historical data about the early Spanish mission, as well as the diseases that ravaged the indigenous populations.

He caught his reflection in the darkened windows. A middle-aged man with thinning hair, an expanding waistline, and desperation in his eyes.

"Who are you kidding?" he muttered. His last three books had barely covered his alimony payments, and the speaking circuit had all but dried up. "You need this."

But could he really live with the consequences?

The smart thing would be to tell the hotel's owner, Tara

Jensen. She would be at the banquet dinner, and he could just walk up and tell her about the crypt, the bones. The gold. He could get ahead of this before it spiraled out of his control. Before Jack enacted his plan.

But the gold. God, the gold.

Barclay had recognized the mint marks and the craftsmanship. It was Spanish colonial era, probably mid-eighteenth century. The find could set him up for life. No more churning out mass-market books, no more speaking at second-rate conferences. He could finally finish his magnum opus about the lost missions of the American Southwest and regain his prestige in the community.

One more drink for courage. The tiny bottle trembled in Barclay's grip as he poured.

A knock at the door made him jump, splashing whiskey onto his sleeve. "Mr. Turner? Your presence is requested for the banquet."

"Yes, yes, coming!"

He dabbed at the wet spot with a tissue, cursing under his breath. He couldn't be late. Jack would be suspicious, and he wanted no more of the man's attention, especially as he was still unsure whether he would speak to Tara.

Barclay hurried out of his room and along to the grand dining room, crowned with its magnificent dome.

He accepted a glass of champagne from a server, trying not to gulp it down as he took his assigned seat, nodding mechanically at his dinner companions.

"Mr. Turner," the woman beside him gushed, "I just loved your book about the Lost Dutchman's Mine! How do you do your research?"

Barclay pasted on his public smile, the one he'd perfected at countless book signings. "Oh, you know, it's all about digging deep." His laugh sounded hollow even to his own ears. "Following the threads of history, looking for patterns, seeking primary sources, and, of course, visiting the locations in person." He reached for his glass, lifting it so a server came to replenish it. "There's no substitute for boots on the ground."

Across the room, Barclay noticed Tara Jensen working the crowd with practiced ease.

He should tell her about the discovery. Right now.

His chair scraped against the floor as he pushed it back and started to rise.

"But Mr. Turner," his dinner companion persisted, grabbing his arm, "what about your next book? Can you give us a hint?"

"I…" His reply caught in his throat as Barclay watched Tara laugh at something a guest said.

Would she even believe him? A washed-up academic crying wolf about ancient Spanish gold? Jack would deny everything, probably have him thrown out into the storm. And then what? Back to scraping by on diminishing advances for his books, his scholarly reputation still in tatters?

"It's actually about a Spanish mission in Death Valley," he managed. "The untold story of—"

Outside, a flash of lightning illuminated the storm clouds, now directly overhead. Thunder followed immediately, so close it rattled the glasses.

Barclay sat back down and took another gulp of wine, turning to the woman next to him with practiced charm. He would wait, perhaps talk to Tara later. For now, he had an enthusiastic audience for his stories, and that was rare enough to warrant his full attention.

* * *

Jack stood at the edge of the grand dining room, his back to the wall where he could survey both exits and the bank of security monitors partially hidden behind an ornamental screen. The position gave him optimal coverage while still keeping him separate from the bloated display of wealth spread before him.

Marble floors gleamed beneath designer heels that cost more than a month's worth of ammunition. Glasses clinked as the wealthy guests celebrated this authentic desert experience, while maintaining a safe distance from any actual survival situations.

But their facade would come crashing down when the veneer of civilization cracked. One sustained crisis, one broken supply chain, and these pampered parasites would turn on each other like starving dogs.

Jack gave a smile as he cataloged their weaknesses.

The Hollywood B-lister star two tables over could barely lift his glass, and those soft hands had never known genuine work. The socialite by the window wore shoes that would cripple her after less than a mile of actual walking.

And Maxwell Carver-Scott, for all his billions, was just another old man trying to buy immortality with young blood and delusion.

None of them saw what was inevitably coming to this country.

The signs were everywhere if you were paying attention. Civil unrest simmering in major cities, new virus variants emerging from labs, supply chains stretched to breaking point. These people would be the first to fall when it all came apart.

But Jack would be ready — and now it might be sooner than expected. The sale of the snake venom would have added a nice bump to his preparations, but he would get more from the celebrity chef anyway. Six thousand per viper, plus another five for discretion. Forty-one thousand in total. Jack suppressed a smile at the successful pivot.

Of course, he should have insisted on payment upfront, instead of waiting until after the banquet. But Rafael wasn't going anywhere, not in this storm.

Jack looked at his watch. He had time to get back down and make sure the chef paid before heading into the tunnels with Barclay, which would be the bigger payday of the night.

The gold below might well set him up permanently. His fence in Vegas didn't ask questions as long as his percentage was fair. The payment would be enough to finish the compound's defense systems and still have plenty left for additional stockpiles.

Tonight, Jack would get out of here, and he couldn't wait to see the back of this lot — as long as everything went to plan.

He checked on the writer.

Barclay sat talking to some puffed-up woman in her fifties. She was clearly making eyes at him, and he leaned into her, touching her arm as he told his stories, eyes bright with wine. Jack frowned. The man was a drunk, and that made for a loose tongue. After they loaded up the maintenance truck tonight... well, the desert had swallowed plenty of secrets before. Jack just had to make it through a few more hours.

He scanned the room with practiced efficiency, maintaining vigilance for threats.

Tara circled between tables, playing the perfect hostess. Casey stood near the service entrance, looking out of place in this environment, wearing a black dress that could almost be practical. And Simone...

Jack's jaw tightened as he fixed on the Carver-Scott table. Simone wore a fitted sheath dress the color of aged champagne, cut to emphasize curves still impressive despite the years. She leaned toward Maxwell occasionally, performing the role of attentive wife with practiced precision, though Jack caught the calculated nature of each gesture. She had always been a good actress.

He had been briefly tempted to give in to her spa invitation earlier, but he wasn't a young security guard anymore, and she wasn't a struggling actress. If he took a woman into his compound, it would be someone younger and stronger. Someone who understood what was coming instead of clinging to fading beauty and a wealthy, aging husband.

A husband who looked increasingly sick this evening, his complexion waxy beneath his tan, a fine sheen of sweat on his forehead despite the controlled temperature of the room.

Simone's fingers trembled slightly as she reached for her wine glass. The distress in her expression seemed genuine enough, but Jack had watched her perform too many times before. There was something off. A tension in her shoulders, a flicker in her eyes that didn't match her concerned demeanor. An actress who had memorized her lines but couldn't quite nail the emotion.

He was still watching when Simone raised a hand to summon Tara to their table, the gesture carrying both urgency and the imperious privilege of wealth.

* * *

Tara plastered a smile on her face as she walked over to the Carver-Scotts' table. Beneath her designer dress her heart hammered out a desperate rhythm of please-hold-together, please-hold-together even as Simone beckoned her with elegant urgency.

"Maxwell's not feeling well. The starter. Was there shellfish in it? He's allergic."

Tara's heart stuttered even as her face remained professionally concerned. She knew every dietary restriction, every allergy, every preference of her high-profile guests, and she made sure her kitchen staff knew them too.

"I can assure you there was no shellfish." She layered warmth and authority into her voice. "Our kitchen maintains the strictest protocols for allergens, and of course, it's not local, so we wouldn't use it, anyway."

She glanced at Maxwell, noting how he pressed his hand against his chest, the sheen of sweat on his brow more pronounced now. "It's likely too soon after serving for any food reaction, anyway. Perhaps the dry atmosphere? The desert air can affect people differently."

Even as she spoke, Tara's mind raced through contingencies. The resort's medical kit was fully stocked. Three of her staff were EMT certified. But if something went seriously wrong—

A sudden gust of wind rattled the dome windows with perfect dramatic timing.

No helicopter could fly in this, and the nearest hospital was hours away by ground transport. Even without the storm, the roads were treacherous at night. With zero visibility, there was no chance of getting out.

"Should we send for a doctor?" Simone asked, her carefully maintained facade cracking. "Surely you must have one on call?"

"Let's not jump to conclusions," Tara soothed. "I'll have our medical staff do a discreet check. And of course, we'll monitor the situation closely."

She gestured to one of her most trusted servers. "Please ask David to stop by the Carver-Scotts' table. Quietly." David was their most experienced EMT, capable of assessing a situation without drawing attention.

Tara deployed her most reassuring smile as she turned back to Simone. "I'm sure it's just the storm affecting him. The pressure changes can be quite dramatic." She touched Simone's arm lightly, the gesture calculated to convey confidence and care. "Try the Château d'Yquem with dessert. I had it brought up specially. The '97 is showing beautifully."

As Tara turned to walk away, Maxwell coughed.

The sound was harsh. Ragged. Wrong.

Tara spun back around.

Maxwell pressed a napkin to his mouth, the silver thread

catching the light. He waved off Simone's concern with his free hand, but Tara saw how his fingers trembled. The man who had built empires with those hands and shaped the future with each decisive gesture now seemed unable to control his shaking.

Surely just a gulp of wine gone down wrong, Tara told herself, her mind already calculating damage control. Just the dry desert air that stripped moisture from everything it touched. Just—

Another cough, this one deeper, wetter.

The sound reminded her of her grandmother's last days in the hospital. A terrible liquid rattle that meant things were breaking down inside.

Maxwell doubled over, his designer suit straining as his body convulsed with racking coughs, his face gray as he fought for breath.

A ripple of awareness moved through the other guests.

Chairs scraped against marble as people shifted away, their instincts warring with social propriety. Their gazes darted between Maxwell's suffering and the nearest exits, the hands reaching instinctively for phones that couldn't even connect to the outside world.

As Tara looked around desperately for David, the storm's violence increased, sand hitting the glass dome like handfuls of thrown gravel.

The sound drew attention upward, away from the drama unfolding below.

The wind found some microscopic gap in the dome's seals, creating an eerie whistling harmony with Maxwell's labored breathing.

A crack appeared in one of the glass panes, the fissure spreading with terrible purpose.

"We have medical help on the way," Tara called out with a practiced tone of calm authority. "If everyone could please give Mr. Carver-Scott some space—"

Lightning fractured overhead.

The lights flickered. Just for a moment, but long enough to send a spike of terror through Tara's chest. Her fingers curled into fists, perfectly manicured nails digging into her palms.

They couldn't lose power. Not now.

Not with her potential investor dying in front of everyone, not with the storm tearing her life's work apart like a hungry beast. The backup generators should kick in, but they'd been acting up lately. Another maintenance cost she'd deferred as the bills piled up.

Maxwell coughed again, this time bringing up an alarming amount of blood.

The spray speckled Simone's designer dress, the crimson drops spreading out against the pale silk.

"He needs a hospital." Simone's voice was sharp with barely controlled panic. "Now!"

But Tara knew it was impossible. The storm had cut them off completely. No roads, no helicopters, no hope of evacuation until it passed.

The lights flickered again, longer this time.

In the momentary darkness, lightning split the sky above the dome.

The flash caught a spreading network of cracks above, transforming the fissures into rivers of fire running through the glass.

"Everyone, get out — now!" Jack's command shattered whatever remained of social restraint.

The room erupted into panic.

* * *

As the dining room dissolved into pandemonium, Barclay caught sight of Jack. Even in the maelstrom of sand and breaking glass, the security chief's face remained impassive, professional. He was entirely focused on the scene before him, and the man's cold efficiency sent a chill down Barclay's spine, reminding him of their agreement in the crypt.

But the chaos presented an opportunity. This was his chance.

Barclay slipped away from his table in the chaotic first wave of retreat, leaving behind blood and sand and screams.

His dinner companion's voice faded into the cacophony as she called after him, but he didn't look back even as the sound of shattering glass and panic pursued him down the hallway.

The corridor to his room felt longer than before, each step taking him further from the destruction but closer to his own moral compromise.

The rigorous academic he'd once been would be appalled at his next moves, but that version of himself hadn't faced bankruptcy and professional exile.

He needed his backpack, the map, and his camera. Proper documentation could be his salvation if this all went wrong. Evidence that he had tried to preserve the site's historical significance, even as he plundered it. The hypocrisy of his position wasn't lost on him, but Barclay pushed the thought away.

Survival first, ethics later.

CHAPTER 19

THE CRACKS SPREAD WITH impossible speed, each
new fissure branching into dozens more like lightning
frozen in glass.

The dome transformed into a deadly kaleidoscope
suspended above their heads, catching and fracturing the
storm's light.

Another flash of lightning. The scene turned stark white
for a heartbeat.

The thunder that followed rolled through the building
like the voice of judgment, so deep Tara felt it in her bones.

The vibration reached the weakened dome, sending
tremors through the compromised structure.

The first piece broke free — a massive shard near the
apex that seemed to hang suspended for an eternal moment.

Gravity claimed it, and the entire structure began to fail.

The shards began as a deadly snow of smaller pieces that
glittered as they descended. Larger sections followed, jagged
sheets of glass falling in a cascade, thousands of edges striking thousands of edges as the fragments collided on their
way down.

Lightning flashed again, and in the stark illumination,
Tara saw the full scope of destruction.

The entire dome was coming apart, dissolving into a

curtain of razor-sharp shards that would shred everything beneath. The glass caught the light as it fell, creating a moment of terrible beauty.

Tara darted to the closest interior wall, protected by a decorative overhang, watching as her perfect world dissolved into glittering chaos. Time seemed to slow, each shard catching the last flickers of light as they fell.

Beautiful, she thought absurdly. Like diamonds raining from the sky.

The desert rushed in, and the heart of the storm now swirled inside the elegant dining room, transforming it into chaos.

Tara stood transfixed, unable to move, gasping at the scale of the destruction as guests screamed, bloodied and broken as pieces of glass rained down from the collapsed dome.

"Under the tables!" Jack's command fought against the storm's howl, but the wind devoured his words.

The emergency sirens blared out, adding their mechanical screech to human terror to create a primal cacophony, a wall of sound.

Tara could only watch as Grace Lin dived beneath a table, her designer dress ruined by glass and sand and blood. The influencer grabbed one of the Santa Fe artists on the way down — what was her name? Ellen? Helen? — pulling her to relative safety.

The taste of the storm filled Tara's mouth, mineral-sharp and ancient, and the blowing sand burned in her eyes. She blinked rapidly, trying to get her bearings.

Visibility had dropped to nearly nothing, and moving shapes appeared and vanished in the maelstrom — stumbling guests, running staff, all turned into wraithlike figures by the swirling debris.

A deep, tortured groan of metal under stress came from above.

Tara's heart seized as the implications hit her.

The glass dome was not purely aesthetic. It was integral to the building's support structure. She remembered the architectural meetings, the warnings about load-bearing requirements, but she'd been so focused on the visual impact, and creating something spectacular…

"Move!" Terror gave her strength as she shoved the nearest guest toward the emergency stairs, though she could barely see its green light through the haze. "Everyone out! Now!"

Another beam creaked overhead, the sound triggering a memory from construction. 'The dome distributes the load evenly,' the architect explained. 'Remove it, and the entire structure becomes unstable.' Tara had nodded along, more concerned with aesthetics than engineering.

The lights flickered again, staying dark longer this time before the emergency systems engaged.

The motion of the sand swirled by the howling wind created shifting patterns and the blood-red emergency lighting cast crimson shadows, transforming faces into nightmare masks.

"Follow the emergency lights!" Casey's voice carried surprisingly well, maintaining its professional edge even in disaster.

While most guests ran, some remained frozen, injured and bloody, or paralyzed by shock and fear.

Maxwell Carver-Scott remained at his table, blood now mixed with sand on his expensive shirt. Simone tried to pull him up, but he seemed unable to move.

The wind changed direction suddenly, creating a vortex of sand and debris in the center of the room. Tables lifted off the ground, their contents becoming deadly projectiles. Glasses shattered against the walls and cutlery flew like shrapnel.

"Please move," Tara whispered, though no one could hear her over the storm's rage. "Please."

The wind intensified, bringing with it a peculiar howl that the local Timbisha had reminded her of during construction. "The desert has its own voice," the tribal elder said. "And it doesn't like being caged." She dismissed it as superstition then, along with so much of her heritage, focused only on her vision of conquering this harsh landscape.

Now that desert voice filled her failing structure as the sand scoured everything it touched, stripping away the veneer of civilization as easily as it stripped paint from metal.

The sound built to a crescendo that felt like pressure in her skull — wind and sirens and screaming metal and human voices all combining into a wall of pure chaos. The air seemed to vibrate with it, making her bones ache and her teeth rattle.

In the crimson light, the swirling patterns looked almost alive, as if spirits of the desert danced through her ruined dreams, celebrating her downfall.

Something sharp struck Tara's forehead, sending warm blood trickling into her eyes. The salt sting of it mixed with sand and tears as she fought her way across the debris-strewn floor toward the Carver-Scotts. She couldn't lose her biggest potential investor, not like this. Not when everything else was literally crumbling around her.

A flash of lightning. The spear of purple-white split the storm-dark sky and struck the Sanctuary's heart.

The impact sent a shockwave through the building that Tara felt deep in her bones. For one suspended moment, she thought the strike had somehow missed, that the danger was past.

But then the eco-wooden beams — sustainably sourced, traditionally blessed by a Timbisha elder — burst into flames.

The fire spread with unnatural speed, as if the wood had merely been waiting for this chance to revel.

Orange tongues of flame danced along exposed beams

as a grinding crack split the air, the sound of stressed metal and concrete giving up the fight against gravity.

The eastern section of the roof, weakened by the lightning strike, folded inward like wet paper, dropping to the ground — and taking with it one side of the room.

Three tables of guests — including most of the Santa Fe artists who'd been so eager for authentic indigenous wisdom — disappeared into the void as the floor beneath them crumbled away. Their screams were cut off with terrible suddenness, replaced by the wet thud of falling debris.

"Everyone move!" Jack's voice cut through the chaos. "Get out. NOW!"

Pure panic consumed the remaining guests, animal instinct replacing civilized behavior as they scrambled to escape.

As the fire spread, the sprinklers finally activated.

But instead of the expected deluge, they produced only a weak trickle of dark water, which quickly dripped to nothing.

Tara's stomach clenched as she remembered Casey's report of contaminated water. Had it clogged the system up altogether?

The fire roared louder and smoke billowed, turning the room into a hellish landscape of shadow. Guests stumbled past her, designer clothes torn and bloodied, their faces transformed by fear and injury into masks of primal terror.

Another section of roof groaned overhead as the smoke grew thicker, making every breath a struggle.

As the flames roared closer, Tara remembered her grandmother's warning about the desert: 'Some debts can only be paid in blood.'

CHAPTER 20

GRACE HUDDLED BENEATH THE table, her shoulder pressed against Helen, who clutched her arm so tight the turquoise rings pressed deep into her skin.

Another section of the wall collapsed with a thunderous roar as jagged shards of glass skittered across the floor.

Grace pushed herself back under the shelter as far as possible, but there was no way this would be safe for long. "We have to move. The fire's spreading so fast."

The flames advanced with terrible purpose, consuming the eco-friendly wooden beams that she had considered showcasing in her posts just hours before. #EcoLuxury #SanctuaryStyle.

The idea turned to ash as she watched the sustainable certification literally go up in smoke.

An acrid smell wafted over them — not just burning wood, but something chemical that made her throat constrict.

Grace frowned. She recognized that smell.

Her sabotage. The granules that turned the water system black and thickened the liquid to sludge.

Her attempt at environmental justice now ensured there was no defense against the fire.

"Oh god," she choked out. "What have I done?"

Horror clawed at her chest as the smoke twisted before her. The elaborate patterns would have made stunning content, backlit by flames that painted everything in a hellish palette of orange and red. Like one of those immersive art installations she was paid thousands to promote — except this inferno was terrifyingly real. This wasn't content. This was consequence.

Through the chaos, Grace caught glimpses of faces she'd studied earlier at dinner, cataloging them for potential networking opportunities. Those same faces were now transformed by primal terror. A woman in Valentino stumbled past, her designer dress in tatters, blood and mascara running down her dust-streaked face. The scene could be a perfect metaphor for the collapse of civilization — exactly the kind of statement her eco-collective would celebrate.

"Get to the exit!" Casey's voice cut through the chaos. "Everyone move toward the emergency lights!"

But many guests remained frozen, paralyzed by the realization that their wealth and status meant nothing in the face of nature's destruction.

Grace's heart stuttered in her chest. The flames had spread in an almost perfect circle, consuming everything in their path with democratic indifference. The sustainably sourced furniture, the indigenous artwork, all the carefully curated elements of eco-luxury that Grace had once promoted with such conviction.

Movement caught her attention through the thickening smoke.

Maxwell Carver-Scott, the tech billionaire, stumbled toward the exit, his body racked with convulsions. He clutched at the wall as blood sprayed from his mouth, leaving crimson droplets suspended in the light of the flames before they fell to the marble floor.

As the billionaire's wife rushed after her husband, their daughter Isla's scream pierced the air. Pure animal fear, stripping away all pretense of civilization.

The girl bolted away from the chaos, her long hair streaming behind her as she disappeared into the smoke.

Grace had photographed her earlier, thinking what a perfect example she was of inherited privilege. Now all she could see was a scared child running for her life.

"Isla!" Simone's voice cracked as she tried to follow, but Maxwell's hand shot out, grabbing her arm as another violent convulsion racked his body.

Casey, the adventure guide, sprinted past Grace's hiding place in pursuit of Isla. Her movements were purposeful even in the chaos, as she darted around the debris and destruction. The woman's practical black dress and sensible shoes, which Grace had mentally critiqued earlier as hopelessly unstylish, now seemed like battle armor compared to the designer outfits that hindered everyone else's escape.

As Grace watched Casey disappear into the smoke, she wished she had that kind of clarity of purpose, that kind of decisive action.

Instead, she remained frozen under a table, her eco-friendly hemp designer dress now soaked with sweat and fear. She wanted to be a warrior for the environment, but warriors ran toward danger, not away from it.

The irony wasn't lost on her. She had cultivated a perfect image of fearless activism, staging photos at protests and rallies, and she was now paralyzed when real courage was needed.

Her phone sat useless in her clutch bag. Grace couldn't document this moment, unable to transform this horror into carefully filtered content for her fans. But perhaps this was the most authentic she'd ever been.

No filters. No crafted captions. Just the raw truth of what her actions had helped create — chaos, destruction, and the terrified scream of a frightened child echoing in her ears.

The flames spread faster now, eating up the beams, desiccated by the dry desert air. They would reach Maxwell and Simone within seconds.

Grace took a deep breath. She could still make a difference.

She stood, teetering in her heels, and lunged for a fire extinguisher mounted on a nearby wall. Her fingers, used to holding phones for perfect selfie angles, scrabbled at the release catch.

"Come on, come on!" The metal burned her hands, the heat from the approaching flames making it almost too hot to touch.

But she kept trying.

This was her chance to help, to do something real instead of performing for likes.

The extinguisher came free, nearly overbalancing her. It was heavier than she expected, and her arms trembled as she turned to face the inferno.

But as she stared at the device, reality crashed in.

She had no idea how to use it.

All those carefully staged photos of her "adventuring," all those sponsored posts about emergency preparedness, and she'd never actually learned the basics of fire safety.

"How do I—" Her hands shook as she fumbled with the nozzle.

The flames crept closer, their heat a physical force against her skin.

Finally, something clicked, and the extinguisher came to life with a hiss of compressed air.

A white chemical spray arced out, looking pathetically small against the wall of fire it faced. Grace tried to remember scenes from movies — how did the heroes do this? She aimed at the base of the flames, but it seemed to make no difference.

The extinguisher sputtered, coughed, and died.

"No, please!" She shook it frantically, but nothing happened.

The fire advanced, and Grace stood helpless before it, the useless extinguisher dropping from her exhausted grip.

A scream ripped through the air behind her.

She spun to see Helen now thrashing on the floor, her clothes ablaze.

Grace ripped the cashmere shawl from her shoulders — an $800 piece she'd been paid to promote as 'adventure luxury wear' — and threw herself down beside the burning woman.

The floor's heat seared through her clothes, but she ignored it, beating at the flames, rolling Helen to try to put out the fire.

It fought back, catching her hands and her arms, searing her skin. The pain was real in a way nothing in her curated life had ever been.

Grace screamed but didn't stop, smothering the flames with desperate determination. The smell of burning flesh — her own and Helen's — filled her senses.

The flames finally died and Grace helped Helen to her feet, supporting her weight as they staggered away from the inferno. Tears streamed down her face, washing away the soot and smoke stains.

She had wanted to expose the hotel's environmental hypocrisy and strike a blow against the wealthy elite who were destroying the planet. Instead, she had helped create this hell of flames and blood and screaming.

All her carefully constructed posts about "eating the rich" felt hollow now as she watched real people fight for their lives.

Something burned her eyes — smoke or maybe tears. Either way, she could no longer tell where the performance ended and reality began.

* * *

The wind howled outside, and sand pelted against the windows as Barclay grabbed his backpack from the closet and shoved in his flashlight, notebook, gloves, and camera with the low-light lens.

The map lay where he'd hidden it, folded between the pages of his dog-eared copy of *Lost Missions of the American Southwest*, his own book written before the Peruvian scandal. As he picked the book up, the pages fell open to a passage: 'We are not treasure hunters, but custodians of history.' His own words mocked him now.

He slammed the book shut, just as a deafening crash came from the main section of the hotel.

The building shuddered, and Barclay rushed to the window.

A gust of wind tore the curtain of sand apart for a second, and he saw the magnificent glass dome, the resort's crown jewel, was now a gaping wound in the shell of the building

Wind and sand poured in through the breach, and in the growing darkness, he saw flames lick the exposed wooden beams.

The implications hit him.

The fire would spread through the hotel's infrastructure, following the electrical conduits and air conditioning ducts. The basement, the ruins, everything would be threatened.

The Spanish gold, the historical artifacts, the indigenous remains. All of it could be lost forever.

The site needed to be documented before it was destroyed. The academic in him, the part that still believed in preservation and proper methodology, screamed that he had a duty to history.

But the gold whispered louder.

Even just a handful of coins from that chest represented freedom from debt, redemption in the academic community, and a chance to rebuild his reputation. If the fire reached the basement, if the ceiling collapsed, all of it could be lost. The bones would mingle with modern ruins, the artifacts crushed beyond recognition, and the gold — his salvation — would be buried forever.

He had to choose. Document the site and preserve what knowledge he could, or grab what he could carry and run. History versus survival. Ethics versus opportunity. The man he had been versus the man he might become.

Barclay shouldered his backpack and yanked open his door.

The corridor was hazy with smoke, emergency lights casting everything in a hellish red glow. The fire alarm's shriek competed with the storm's howl.

Other guests hurried past him, wounded and bleeding, confused and frightened. Barclay ignored them, pushing past toward the service stairs.

The basement access door was supposed to be locked, but the hotel's security systems had failed along with the power.

The handle turned easily under his trembling fingers.

The temperature dropped as he descended into the basement. His flashlight beam caught dust motes dancing in the air, stirred up by the vibrations from above.

The distant crash of breaking glass and groaning metal reminded him that time was running out.

He pushed aside the shelving unit that barely disguised access, and the tunnel mouth gaped before him. A throat of darkness that swallowed his flashlight beam.

Barclay hesitated at the threshold as another crash came from above.

Dust and small debris rained down from the ceiling as the hotel's structure weakened further under the dual assault of storm and fire.

He didn't have much time.

"Forgive me," he whispered, unsure whether he asked forgiveness from God, from the dead — or from his own conscience.

He stepped into the darkness as the storm raged on above.

CHAPTER 21

As Maxwell reached the wall, his legs gave way beneath him. His vision wavered and his hearing dulled as the grand dining room descended into chaos. Screams echoed as roaring flames devoured the wooden beams overhead.

The heat was extreme, and his watch buzzed with warnings about his elevated body temperature, his arrhythmic heart, his labored breathing. Maxwell tried to focus on the tiny display — his vitals had always anchored him — but the screen was just a blur.

Another convulsion racked him. Blood filled his mouth. So much blood.

He spat it out, and some part of his mind stood outside of the reality of it all, unable to process what was happening even as his body shook with pain.

He was Maxwell Carver-Scott. He had reengineered his body under the supervision of the best longevity doctors. Every cell had been optimized, every system enhanced. The young blood treatments alone cost many millions. He had turned back his biological clock. He could not be sick.

He could not be dying.

Another convulsion seized him. His muscles, maintained by carefully calibrated hormone treatments and daily workouts, locked into a painful spasm. The feeling was alien, wrong — like his body was being rewritten on a cellular level. The blood treatments were supposed to rejuvenate and restore. Instead, something was breaking him down from the inside out.

Through the dark spots dancing across his vision, he saw the flames advance toward him, yet he couldn't move.

"Maxwell!" Simone's desperate voice cut through his fading consciousness.

He looked at his wife, chosen for her youth and beauty, of which there were only echoes now. The smoke cast strange shadows across her face, but even through his dimming vision, he caught something in her expression.

Behind the terror, beneath the mask of concern, there was something else. Something he recognized in himself just before he closed a valuable deal. Could it be satisfaction at a guaranteed outcome?

The realization hit him.

The blood. The treatment she had so carefully prepared was tainted.

Isla's scream pierced the chaos. She bolted away, disappearing into the smoke.

Simone tried to run after her. Maxwell snarled and locked his fingers around Simone's wrist with desperate strength even as the adventure guide Casey rushed away after their daughter.

He would not be abandoned. Not now. Not like this. If this was to be his end, she would not escape the consequences.

His grip tightened, and he felt her delicate bones shift.

"Maxwell, please," she whispered. "Isla—"

"Get me out of here." The words came out in a bloody spray, staining her skin, dripping down her dress, as another convulsion hit, driving him to his knees.

* * *

"Isla!" Casey shouted as she watched the girl run away from her parents and dart between fallen beams, flames casting wild shadows that made her slight form flicker like a desert mirage.

The heat was overwhelming and sparks rained down, catching in Casey's hair as she tracked Isla's movement through the chaos.

The girl hesitated as she found herself surrounded by a wall of burning debris, the carefully curated furniture now transformed into a blazing barrier. Casey calculated angles, looking for a safe path through.

"Stay there! I'll come to you!" But the inferno's roar swallowed her words.

Isla turned, her face illuminated by the flames; her features twisted with a terror that sent Casey straight back to that cave in the heart of the Mendip Hills, to another child's desperate eyes.

Not again. Never again.

But before Casey could reach her, Isla spotted a gap in the flames and dove through. She darted down what was left of the stairs into the collapsed lobby, and disappeared into the smoke beyond.

The burning timber shifted, cutting off any chance of following.

The heat seared Casey's lungs as she spun around, searching for another route. The service corridor and stairwell looped around and down to the same area.

She ran, slipping on the marble made treacherous by blood and broken glass, as the emergency lights strobed above.

Casey burst through the exit door into the storm.

Sand scoured every inch of her exposed skin as the wind howled.

"Isla!" she shouted, but the storm swallowed her words.

Visibility was almost zero, the world reduced to swirling

red-brown darkness broken by occasional flashes of lightning. The hot wind battered her, each gust threatening to sweep her off her feet.

Casey pushed on, remembering Isla's fascination with the desert out in the buggy. The girl had an instinct for this landscape that went beyond her privileged upbringing. Perhaps it would help her now.

At least Casey clung to that hope as she pushed through the carefully maintained gardens, now a churning maelstrom in the wind. Palm trees bent sideways, their fronds thrashing back and forth while desert plants — agave, barrel cactus, Joshua trees — stood like dark sentinels in the gloom. Sand built against their bases, creating new dunes that shifted and flowed with each fresh gust.

Casey's feet sank into the loose sand, each step requiring conscious effort. The howling wind and stinging sand made it hard to navigate as she rounded the corner toward where Isla must have emerged from the dome.

Then she heard a sound — a high, thin scream. Isla.

* * *

Maxwell's consciousness flickered like the flames consuming the grand dining room.

This wasn't how it was supposed to end. He had so many plans. Quantum computing breakthroughs, neural uploading research, outer space initiatives. He was meant to live long enough to see humanity's next evolution, to guide it with his wealth and vision.

The smoke burned his lungs, lungs that had been treated with stem cell therapy, that should be as efficient as a twenty-year-old's.

His heart hammered arrhythmically against his ribs, each beat shooting pain through his chest.

Through the strobe of emergency lights and flame-cast shadows, he saw other guests fleeing. Primitive terror transformed their faces, all their wealthy sophistication stripped away by survival, reducing them to desperate animals by fire and fear.

He would not be like them. He was Maxwell Carver-Scott. He had built empires, broken monopolies, reshaped the fabric of society. He would not die here, choking on his own blood before being burned to death on the edge of the desert.

"Help me up," he commanded his wife, forcing authority into his failing voice.

Simone hesitated, her eyes darting out to where Isla had disappeared, with the guide right behind her.

The flames were closer now, their heat blistering his skin.

"The guide will find her. Help me up, now!" The words cost him, bringing up another gout of blood, but it carried enough authority to make her comply.

Simone gripped his arm, her strength surprising him as she hauled him upright. The world spun, and he tasted bile mixed with blood in his throat.

But he was standing. He was fighting.

"The suite," he managed.

They staggered through smoke-filled corridors, down the emergency stairs, past fleeing guests and panicked staff. Every step was agony, his muscles refusing to coordinate properly, but he forced himself on, leaning heavily on Simone.

His vision tunneled, focusing only on the next step, the next breath.

He would survive this. He would find out what she had done to his treatments, what poison she had used to destroy his optimized system.

Then he would make her pay.

Not just with divorce, but with complete destruction. He

would erase her so thoroughly that even his worst enemies would seem fortunate by comparison.

The suite's door materialized through the smoke-filled corridor, wavering in his failing vision.

Maxwell's legs trembled beneath him, the muscles he'd spent thousands of hours and millions of dollars maintaining now betraying him with every step. He forced himself on. He was Maxwell Carver-Scott. He did not succumb to weakness.

Simone's arm around his waist felt both supportive and threatening, the touch of someone who had planned his destruction with intimate knowledge of his vulnerabilities.

The keycard shook in her hand as she unlocked the door, and they stumbled in, the luxury sanctuary now rendered alien by his dimming sight. Through the floor-to-ceiling windows, the storm had transformed the million-dollar view into an apocalyptic wasteland, as red-brown sand whirled like blood in water.

His legs gave out as they reached the bed and Maxwell collapsed onto the imported Egyptian cotton sheets — twelve hundred thread count, at his insistence.

Blood sprayed from his mouth as another convulsion hit, staining the fabric a deep crimson. The bitter chemical taste was stronger now. Undeniable.

His tongue felt numb, and the paralysis was spreading.

"Simone," he forced out between wet, gasping breaths. The words brought up more blood, but he needed to see her reaction. "You... did this."

Her eyes widened, just slightly, but he hadn't built an empire worth billions without learning to read people's tells. The flash of panic, quickly masked by practiced concern. The micro-expression of satisfaction, hastily hidden.

After three marriages, he should have known better than to trust a beautiful woman with his life.

He coughed again, the sound wet and thick with blood.

Simone backed away from the bed. The distance between them grew with each step — not just physical space, but years of carefully hidden resentment finally showing through her perfect mask.

"I'll get help," she said, but they both knew it was a lie.

Maxwell tried to reach for his phone, but his arms felt leaden, unresponsive.

The room spun around him as a wave of dizziness hit.

Beneath his physical collapse, his mind fixed on revenge. He would survive this. He had the best doctors on call, experimental treatments available in exclusive labs. Once he recovered, she would pay for every drop of tainted blood.

The last thing Maxwell saw before his vision blurred completely was Simone silhouetted in the doorway against the smoke beyond.

For a moment, she looked like the young actress he'd first met, before he remade her into the perfect corporate wife. Then she stepped through the door and was gone, leaving him alone as his world faded to black.

CHAPTER 22

CASEY RAN TOWARD THE scream, her feet slipping in sand whipped up against her face by the swirling wind.

The storm had transformed the familiar landscape into a wasteland, visibility reduced to mere feet ahead, but her trained eye caught what others might miss. Footprints like ghost impressions in the sand, already half-erased by the relentless wind. The slight depression of a heel, the drag of panicked steps.

They led toward one of the desert gardens, now being systematically destroyed by the storm, as it stripped away the garden's protective layers and exposed the treacherous ground beneath.

Casey followed the screams — and found Isla thrashing in quicksand. The storm had blown sand into the damaged terrain, creating a deadly trap that pulled her deeper with every movement.

"Don't move!" Casey dropped to her knees at the edge of solid ground. "Isla, look at me!"

Isla turned her head and Casey saw the raw fear in her eyes, tears cutting clean tracks through the sand coating her face. Years of wilderness rescue training crystallized into a single, clear thought: this was solvable. Unlike the cave, where stone walls had pressed in with suffocating weight, here she had open sky and proven techniques. Her mind snapped into the familiar pattern: assess, analyze, act. She knew exactly how to handle quicksand. She just had to keep her voice steady and guide Isla through it.

"Casey! Help me, please! I can't get out!" Her voice cracked on the last word, high and thin with panic.

Casey pressed her palms into the edge of the firm ground, anchoring herself. "Listen to me carefully." She pitched her voice above the wind's howl. "Spread your arms out wide, like you're making a snow angel. That's it… Now lean back, slowly. Think of it like floating in a pool. Nice and easy."

Isla's breath came in hitching gasps, but she followed the instructions.

The quicksand pulled at her, but as Casey watched, the girl's weight redistributed more evenly. The desert was merciless, but it followed rules, and physics didn't care about panic or privilege.

"That's great. Now make some little rowing movements with your hands." Casey kept her voice calm, though her own heart raced. "Like you're on a raft and want to get to the side of the pool. Nice and slow."

The wind howled around them, but Isla maintained focus, her eyes locked on Casey's face as she worked her way toward solid ground. Each movement was agonizingly slow, but the sand's hold gradually loosened and Isla inched closer to the edge.

"Almost there." Casey stretched out as far as she dared, her muscles trembling with the strain. The sand below her was solid, but one wrong move and there would be a second victim. "Just a little more."

Isla reached out. Their fingers brushed — slipped in the gritty wind — then caught.

Casey seized Isla's wrist, and with a surge of desperate strength, she heaved backward.

The quicksand fought to keep its prize, but Casey was

stronger, fueled by the ghosts of past failure and her absolute refusal to let history repeat itself.

She pulled until her shoulders screamed in protest, until spots danced at the edges of her vision.

With a sucking sound, Isla came free, and they tumbled back together onto solid ground.

Casey wrapped her arms around the girl, feeling her whole body shake with sobs. The storm raged around them, but in that moment, all Casey could feel was the thundering of two hearts, both still beating.

"I've got you," she whispered into Isla's sand-caked hair. "I've got you. You're safe now."

For a moment, they held each other as the storm raged around them, two insignificant figures in a vast apocalyptic landscape.

Casey pulled back enough to see Isla's face. "We need to get inside and find your parents. Can you stand?"

Isla nodded, even though tears still streamed down her cheeks. Casey helped her up, keeping a firm grip on her hand, and together they turned to face the storm, leaning into the wind as they battled their way back to the hotel.

Lightning flickered, turning the swirling sand into sheets of ghostly purple-white, while thunder cracked overhead and the wind howled.

Through the maelstrom, Casey could see the hotel's outline, the broken dome now transformed by flames into a burning beacon. Smoke poured from where the banquet hall had been. The sight sent fresh urgency through her tired muscles. They had survived the storm and the quicksand, but the inferno ahead presented a new hell. This place was no desert sanctuary anymore.

Casey pulled Isla closer as they approached the nearest entrance, its automatic doors frozen half-open, as smoke spiraled out into the storm. They had no choice. It was their only way in.

Casey half-ran, half-dragged Isla through the smoke-filled corridors toward the exclusive suites.

"Almost there," she rasped, trying not to inhale too deeply as she navigated the hallways. Each breath felt like swallowing fire.

Isla stumbled beside her, coughing as her small hand clutched Casey's with desperation.

They rounded another corner. The Carver-Scott suite lay just ahead, its double doors standing open, framing Simone, who was desperately scanning the corridor.

"Mom!" Isla broke free and ran to her mother.

Simone swept her daughter into her arms and pressed frantic kisses to Isla's sand-caked hair. "I thought… When you ran… I'm so sorry."

She looked over at Casey. "Thank you. Thank you for bringing her back. Come inside, please."

Casey nodded as another wave of smoke rolled through the corridor. The three of them hurried inside and closed the doors.

The sound of choking came from further within.

Maxwell lay in the next room on the massive bed, his body contorted in violent spasms. Blood frothed at his lips. His eyes were open but unseeing, rolled back to show mostly white as another seizure racked him.

Isla caught sight of her father. "Daddy?"

Simone tried to turn her away, but Isla resisted, her face a mask of horror as she watched her father fight for each breath.

Isla reached out one hand toward Casey, her fingers trembling. "Please don't go. I'm scared."

Lightning split the sky outside the suite's floor-to-ceiling windows. The flash turned everything stark white for a heartbeat, followed by thunder that shook the building to its foundations.

Out the windows, Casey could see the fire advancing

along the hotel's exterior, consuming the carefully maintained façade meter by meter. The flames seemed almost alive, reaching with hungry fingers in their direction. It wouldn't be long before it reached these living quarters.

They had to get out of here.

Maxwell coughed again, spraying blood across the sheets even as his body weakened in its convulsions.

Simone pulled Isla closer and looked over at Casey. "What do we do about the fire? Maxwell? Are we safe here?"

"We need to get out of here." Casey kept her voice steady as she watched the flames creep closer outside. The heat was already making the windows creak ominously in their frames. "The basement level has stone walls and concrete foundations. It's our best chance."

Even as she said it, the word basement made Casey's stomach clench and bile rise in her throat. It was underground. Enclosed.

No escape.

Eric's face flashed through her mind. His eyes wide with terror as the cave's darkness pressed in, his voice growing weaker as the oxygen ran out. Her chest tightened, the familiar panic clawing its way up from her gut.

But there was no other option.

"I'll take you down and show you the way." She glanced over at Maxwell's thrashing form. "Then I'll come back for him. It will be quicker if I do two trips."

The lie tasted bitter on her tongue. She could hear the death rattle in Maxwell's throat, the way each breath brought up more gouts of blood. Whatever was killing him was working fast.

But Isla was watching, and the girl needed hope right now. Not the truth. She wouldn't leave if she didn't believe her dad would be safe.

Casey swallowed hard. She could do this. She had to do this.

She reached out to take Isla's hand. "We need to move now, while we still can."

The flames were closer now, their roar almost drowning out Maxwell's wet, desperate gasps. The heat pressed against them like a living thing, hungry and impatient.

Casey squeezed Isla's hand gently. "Stay close to me. Both of you."

She took one last look at Maxwell, then led Isla and Simone out of the suite.

Together, they ran through corridors that were now a maze of fire and smoke. Sparks rained down from burning ceiling tiles, forcing them to dodge and weave.

"This way!" Casey directed them around a fallen light fixture, its wiring still sparking dangerously.

The fire's spread pattern was much worse than it should have been. The flames moved fast, finding paths they shouldn't, consuming materials that should have been fire resistant.

A section of ceiling crashed down behind them.

"Keep moving!" she shouted as Isla whimpered, her grip tightening on Casey's hand.

The memory of Tara's office. Those stacks of unpaid bills, the desperate look in the owner's eyes. How many corners had been cut to keep this place running? The fire-resistant beams burned like kindling, the sprinkler system had failed, and the smoke spread through supposedly sealed corridors. Every safety feature was compromised.

They rounded the last corner to find Jack standing in front of the basement door, his face eerily lit by the flickering emergency lights. He was clearly heading down himself.

He put a hand out as they approached. "Stop! It's not safe down there."

"Nowhere's safe!" Casey snapped back, pulling Isla closer as a wave of heat rolled over them. "The building's going to come down around us, and we can't go outside in that storm. The basement is our only option. Let us through."

A crash from behind them, a roar of flame. The sound of groaning metal filled the air as support beams began to give way.

The ceiling caved in behind them, a cascade of burning debris cutting off any chance of retreat. The heat became unbearable, searing the air.

Simone acted first, shoving past Jack with surprising strength. She pulled Isla with her through the basement door, their footsteps echoing as they hurried down the concrete stairs.

Jack hesitated only a moment before following, turning his back on Casey, his broad shoulders disappearing into the darkness below.

Casey stood rooted in place, fists clenched. Flames advanced all around her, but her feet refused to move. She had promised Isla she would go back for Maxwell, but the inferno behind her made that impossible. In her mind's eye, she could still see his form on the bed, the violent convulsions weakening, blood-flecked foam at his lips. He would be gone before she could reach him — if he wasn't already dead. Another failure, another broken promise, but at least this time the choice had been taken from her by the flames.

She had to go on, and yet the darkness beyond the door made her heart pound and her vision narrow.

It all rushed back. The stone walls closing in, the echo of desperate breathing in confined space, the moment those breaths began to slow and stop. Her chest tightened as panic clawed its way up from her gut.

"Casey?!" Isla called up from below, breaking through Casey's gasps as she tried to control her panic.

She wanted to sink to the ground, put her head in her hands, and pretend none of this was happening. But the flames roared closer, their heat blistering at her from all sides.

She must face her fears down there in the dark — or burn.

CHAPTER 23

THE ACRID SMELL OF smoke seeped down from above, carrying with it the sounds of chaos. Screaming guests, shattering glass, the relentless roar of the storm and fire consuming the hotel as Jack assessed his tactical options.

He should be up there directing people to safety. Their security was his job, after all. But Tara had clearly cut way too many corners with the hotel's construction, and any liability would be on her. Meanwhile, that bastard Barclay had fled, no doubt helping himself to the gold.

Jack needed to get down there — but now there was a complication.

Three complications.

Simone whispered comfort to Isla, their shadows dancing against the basement walls in the flickering emergency lights. Casey stood slightly apart, her eyes wide with the look of someone fighting a primal fear. She grabbed a flashlight and stood holding it like an anchor, as if it would give her stability in the chaos. The British adventure guide might be resourceful in the desert above, but down here in the darkness and basement confines, she was a liability.

"You need to stay here," Jack commanded. "No doubt there will be a rescue team here soon. I need to check whether the foundations are holding, but it's dangerous, so don't follow me further."

He turned to make his way to the storage room that led to the old mission—

A deep boom reverberated through the ceiling, followed by the distinctive crack of supporting beams giving way.

Concrete dust rained down as another section succumbed to the inferno above. The heat intensified, creating a chimney effect that drew hot air down the stairwell.

The basement wouldn't be survivable for long.

Simone pulled Isla toward Jack. "We have to go with you. We can't stay here. It's too dangerous."

Casey's gaze flickered up to the ceiling above. She clearly wanted to stay out here. Her breathing was labored, her footsteps faltering.

Jack remembered her file. A cave incident in England, a dead child. Her fear could work to his advantage. Having the three of them follow him wasn't ideal, but he could use them as a cover for his true objective. If anyone questioned his actions later, he was just helping evacuate guests to safety.

"Okay, follow me, but watch your heads," he warned as the ceiling dipped lower. "And stay close. These tunnels weren't built for tourists. One wrong turn and you'll never find your way out."

The threat wasn't entirely a lie. The Spanish missionaries weren't just saving souls out here in the desert. They were hunting for something more tangible. Gold. Just like the miners that came after them. Just like him.

As they ducked inside, the tunnel's musty air carried the acrid tang of smoke, mixed with the mineral scent of ancient stone.

Jack's mind raced through his options.

The tunnels branched off in multiple directions in some places. He could lose them in the maze if necessary, double back to deal with Barclay, and secure the gold. The women would be found — eventually. He just needed to ditch them at some point.

"Stay close to the walls," he instructed. "And watch your step. The floor isn't even."

His flashlight beam caught glimpses of history in the walls: tool marks from Spanish miners, support beams dark with age, crude crosses carved into the rock by long-dead hands. Then, up ahead, a piece of rotted timber had collapsed from the heat of the fire and partially blocked the path. Beyond it, the tunnel branched in three directions.

Jack knew which way Barclay had gone, and he could almost taste the gold that awaited. This was as good a time as any to leave the dead weight behind, and he could use Casey's fear to help him.

She lagged behind, her footsteps faltering every time the tunnel walls narrowed and pressed closer. Her breathing was shallow and fast. She was barely controlling her panic response. Jack had seen it in green recruits during their first firefight, and those soldiers never lasted. They ran home to their mommies. Pathetic. All he needed to do was amplify Casey's fear and she would do whatever he wanted.

A tremor shook the tunnel, sending a cascade of loose stones pattering down from the ceiling. The fire must be weakening the foundations above them.

Casey gasped, and Isla whimpered, pressing closer to Simone. The sound echoed off the stone walls, multiplying until it seemed to come from all directions.

"Hold up," he commanded, using the beam of his flashlight to illuminate the section where the tunnel branched ahead. "This is where it gets tricky."

He turned to face them, his light casting harsh shadows across their faces. "The tunnels ahead get narrower. Tighter. Darker. It's easy to get lost." He swept the beam across the rough ceiling, where old support timbers groaned under the weight of the earth above. "It's even easier to get crushed if you don't know what you're doing. You might become trapped down here, unable to move. Unable to breathe."

Casey gasped, and the color drained from her face as she stared into the darkness ahead. Her hands clenched and unclenched at her sides.

"Casey" — Jack softened his tone enough to sound concerned rather than commanding — "why don't you stay here with Simone and Isla? Keep them safe while I scout ahead?"

Relief flooded her features. "Yes, yes, of course. We're far enough from the fire here. We don't need to go any deeper." She forced a smile. "We'll stay here, won't we, Isla?"

The girl nodded as she clung to Simone's hand like it was a lifeline. Her mother gave a sharp nod.

"Smart choice," he said, already turning toward the leftmost tunnel. "Stay together. Stay alert. I'll be back once I've checked the route ahead."

The lie was as comfortable as his tactical gear. It should keep them calm and in place while he did what needed to be done. They would wait there, Casey too paralyzed by her fear to venture deeper, and Simone unwilling to risk her daughter in the maze of tunnels. When first responders made it to the hotel, they'd be found. Meanwhile, he would be long gone with the gold.

Another tremor shook the tunnel as Jack strode away, light on his feet now, his boots silent on the stone floor as he rounded the first bend.

Somewhere ahead, Barclay was no doubt sifting through the gold, thinking he could now claim it for himself. But the writer couldn't carry much by himself and he didn't have a vehicle or a fence in Vegas. Jack had all the advantages — and perhaps he didn't even need the writer at all.

As he moved swiftly through the tunnels, Jack reassessed his plan.

His original exit point came out in the hotel, now consumed by fire, but according to the blueprints, there was another way out, emerging near the service road that led behind the adventure garage area and up to the observatory.

He could leave with the gold and never return. There would certainly be no job here after tonight.

As Jack approached the chamber, he heard the scrape of metal on stone, the rustle of fabric, and the labored breathing of someone working at pace.

He turned off his flashlight and let his eyes adjust to the dim glow ahead.

The chamber opened before him, its vaulted ceiling lost in the darkness above. Barclay knelt in the center, his movements frantic as he sorted quickly through the artifacts scattered across the floor. His flashlight cast twisted shadows across the walls of skulls behind him as he picked out the best pieces, and anything small enough to fit in his pack but valuable enough to make it worth the risk.

"You greedy bastard!" Jack crossed the space in three strides, grabbing the strap of Barclay's pack and shoving him back with enough force to send the writer skidding across the uneven floor.

The pack came free, its weight heavy with stolen history.

But Barclay recovered quickly.

He reached for a large reliquary — a gold box meant to hold sacred bones, its surface crusted with dull gems.

He swung it in a wild arc, desperation lending strength.

* * *

Jack tried to duck, but the confined space worked against him.

The reliquary caught him high on the temple, sending an explosion of white-hot pain through his skull.

The impact drove him to one knee, his vision swimming as blood trickled into his eye.

"Son of a—" The curse died as his training took over. He tried to focus, the crypt spinning around him.

Blood pounded in his ears, almost drowning out the sound of Barclay's ragged breathing.

The writer stood over him, the reliquary raised for another blow, its golden surface catching the light like ancient fire.

The ground trembled beneath them as the hotel complex collapsed above, sending a cascade of dust and bone showering down upon them.

Jack blinked hard, forcing his vision to clear.

He could taste blood in his mouth, feel it matting his hair where the reliquary had split his scalp. The pain receded to a dull throb as combat clarity locked in.

Pain was irrelevant. All that mattered was the man standing between him and the gold.

Barclay's hands shook on the reliquary, his shoulders heaving with each breath. Sweat cut through the dust on his face, and his eyes were wide with the terror of someone unused to violence who suddenly found themselves committing it.

"Now what?" Jack's voice came out steady, despite the iron taste of blood on his tongue. "You gonna kill me? Add murder to grave robbery?"

Barclay swallowed hard. "I... I didn't..."

"Didn't what?" Jack shifted his weight slightly, preparing to move. "Didn't think it through? Didn't plan for competition? Or didn't think anyone would care about a few stolen artifacts?"

The beams supporting the crypt ceiling groaned ominously overhead.

More debris rained down, with the sound of bone on metal as pieces of broken skull hit the gold.

Jack rolled left as Barclay swung the heavy reliquary again, feeling the wind of its passage stir his hair. He surged up in one fluid motion, his muscle memory flawless from countless hand-to-hand combat drills. His boots found purchase on the ancient floor as he settled into a fighter's stance, fists raised, weight balanced.

The dizziness receded as they circled each other in the confined space.

Barclay's chest heaved with exertion. Sweat darkened his expensive shirt, and his hands trembled where they gripped the reliquary. But his eyes held the dangerous light of a cornered animal.

"Drop it," Jack growled. "You're not walking out of here with that gold."

"I need this. My reputation, my career. Everything depends on this find, and I know you won't let me keep it."

Barclay swung again, desperation making his attack wild and unpredictable.

The reliquary whistled past Jack's ear as he ducked.

The writer's next swing went wide, the momentum spinning him half around.

Jack saw his opening, started to move — but Barclay recovered faster than he expected, fueled by desperate strength.

The reliquary came at him from an impossible angle, forcing him to dance backward.

His boot caught on something. He stumbled, losing precious inches of maneuvering room in the cramped crypt.

As Jack fought to regain his balance, something shifted in his tactical vest pocket and fell to the floor.

The sound of plastic hitting stone.

Jack's heart seized as the detonator skittered across the floor. The small device tumbled end over end, its black case almost invisible in the shadows.

Time slowed as he watched it roll, visualizing all of the spots where he'd carefully set the charges only hours before. He had placed just enough C4 to bring down the crypt and make the collapse look like structural damage from the storm.

"No—" The word died in his throat as the detonator struck a yellowed femur bone.

The impact drove the primer button down with an audible click. A small red LED pulsed, counting down the minutes until everything they'd fought over would become rubble and dust.

The timer was set for twenty minutes. Long enough to clear the area, short enough to ensure no evidence survived.

Nobody was meant to get hurt, but that was before the hotel collapse, the fire, the three extras who followed Jack in.

His mind raced through scenarios with military precision. The charges were set deep in the crypt walls, positioned to bring down this entire section of the tunnel. Anyone caught in the collapse would be buried under tons of rock — a tragic accident during a natural disaster, their bodies unlikely to ever be found.

Barclay stared at the pulsing LED on the ground, beeping as it counted down each second. "What the hell is that?"

Jack straightened slowly, ignoring the throb of pain where the reliquary had struck.

"That," he said softly, "is the sound of your time running out."

CHAPTER 24

As they huddled in the tunnel, Simone pulled Isla closer. She breathed in the familiar scent of her daughter's shampoo, still detectable beneath smoke and fear. Isla's small body trembled against her own, each shudder a reminder of what was at stake.

"It's going to be okay, sweetheart. We'll make it out of here, I promise." She kept her voice even, with the same tone she used to soothe Isla through nightmares and society parties alike.

A distant crash echoed through the tunnel as the fire and the storm destroyed everything up there on the surface.

Good. Let it all burn.

Let the fire consume every trace of Maxwell's tainted blood, every security camera that might have captured her movements, and every record that could raise questions about his death.

Perhaps this was the best thing that could have happened. They would survive this, and she and Isla would start afresh.

The tunnel walls shuddered and fine debris rained down, coating Simone's shoulders with mineral dust.

"Mommy, I'm scared."

"I know, baby. Just stay close to me." Simone stroked Isla's hair, remembering how Maxwell had criticized its unruly curl just last week. 'Perhaps we should look into permanent straightening treatments,' he'd said, as if their child was another system to be optimized.

A deep rumble shook the passage, and Simone sent up a prayer.

Not to the father god of her childhood Sunday school, but to whatever force ruled this desert, this ancient place that had witnessed so much blood and so many secrets over millennia.

Let my crimes be buried. Let the fire burn everything away. Let my daughter be safe.

The crack of splitting stone interrupted her thoughts.

Simone looked up just as chunks of the tunnel ceiling broke free. Jagged pieces of rock hurtled down.

Instinct took over and Simone threw herself over Isla, covering her daughter's body with her own.

White-hot pain exploded across her back and shoulders as the rocks struck her flesh. The impact drove the air from her lungs, but she bit back her cries.

"Mom!" Isla tried to turn beneath her, but Simone held her still.

"I'm fine," she managed, tasting blood in her mouth. "Stay down."

More rocks clattered around them, but Simone barely registered it through the throbbing agony in her back. Each breath sent fresh spikes of pain through her chest. She had injured something, but she could hide it. She was used to pain.

Pain had taught her to smile through Maxwell's criticism, to remain perfect and polished while he paraded younger assistants through their home, to maintain her mask even as she planned his death.

He had known, at the end. It was written on his face — the rage, the disbelief that she would dare destroy his potential immortality — and she was glad he had realized she was the architect of his destruction.

"The rocks stopped falling," Isla whispered against her chest. "Can we move now?"

Simone forced herself to focus through the pain, to listen past the thunder of her own heartbeat. The rumbling had indeed subsided, leaving only the distant roar of flames.

"Not yet, darling." She kept her voice steady despite the agony screaming through her shoulder. "Let's wait a moment longer and make sure it's safe."

Safe. What a joke. She'd never been safe. Not really.

Not as a struggling actress fending off producers with roving hands, not as Maxwell's perfect wife watching her youth slip away, not now, having finally seized control of her fate.

But Isla would be safe. That's what mattered.

Once this was over, once the fire had burned away their past, she would build something real for her daughter. Something that wasn't measured in stock options and social media impressions.

Simone held Isla close, feeling her daughter's heart beat against her own. Above them, flames devoured the evidence of her sin, and somewhere in their suite, Maxwell's body burned. Assuming he was dead before the flames reached him.

He had to be dead. The alternative didn't bear thinking about.

Casey shifted beside them, her breathing too rapid, too shallow even for the level of danger they were in. Her face was ghost-pale in the dim light, her usual confidence stripped away in the narrow tunnels.

"I don't think the tunnel will hold much longer. We have to go deeper. We can follow Jack's footsteps."

Simone recognized the edge of panic in Casey's voice. The guide was clearly terrified of being underground, but their choices had vanished along with their way back. The collapse meant they had to go on.

Simone struggled to her feet. A fresh wave of pain shot through her and she forced back a cry so as not to alarm Isla.

The rocks had done serious damage. She could feel it in the way her arm hung wrong and the grinding sensation as she moved it. Her fingers tingled with alarming numbness.

"Careful, darling," Simone murmured as her daughter's small hand found hers, squeezing with desperate strength.

Casey led them on, taking the route that Jack had walked before them.

The pain in Simone's shoulder pulsed with every step, spreading tendrils of fire down her arm and across her ribs.

Something was definitely broken, but there was no time to catalog her injuries. No time to think about anything except getting Isla to safety.

Voices echoed up ahead.

Simone recognized Jack's distinctive baritone, rougher now than when they'd been lovers, but still carrying the edge of contained violence that had once thrilled her.

The other voice was unfamiliar, desperate and pleading.

Isla's hand tightened in hers as they rounded a corner, and Simone's breath caught at what the flickering light revealed.

The tunnel opened into a chamber that might once have been sacred. There were bones set into the walls, and carvings of religious symbols, but there was nothing holy about the scene before them.

Jack straddled Barclay's prone form in the center of the chamber, his fists rising and falling with precision.

Each impact produced a wet sound that turned Simone's stomach. So different from the staged fights she remembered from acting classes. This was real violence, primal and terrible.

Gold gleamed in the faltering light around the men. Coins, ceremonial objects, jeweled crucifixes. Gold coins spilled from an open backpack, mixing with something else that made Simone pull Isla closer — bones, dozens of them, scattered across the chamber floor like a charnel house.

Jack rose from his grim work, his chest heaving with exertion, his knuckles stained with blood.

His eyes met Simone's with no trace of their shared past, only a cold calculation that reminded her too much of Maxwell.

"You shouldn't be in here. It's not safe."

Casey took a step into the chamber. "The tunnel has collapsed back there. We had no choice. And it looks like you need reminding that we are supposed to protect the guests, not hurt them. We all need to make it out of here together."

The chamber shuddered as if to emphasize her point, the ancient stone groaning as more debris rained down.

Simone pulled Isla closer, feeling her daughter tremble against her injured side. The pain barely registered now as she assessed the threats surrounding them. Jack's violence, the unstable tunnel behind, and the inferno above that threatened to erase them along with her crime.

CHAPTER 25

THE COLD STONE FLOOR of the crypt pressed against Barclay's face. Blood filled his mouth, and each breath sent daggers of pain through his ribs where Jack's fists had connected. He forced his mind to focus.

The gold. It would be worth it for the gold. He just had to get out of here before the charges went off and the whole place came down.

Two women and a girl stumbled in, and as Jack pulled away, Barclay seized his chance.

He rolled toward the backpack, his fingers scrabbling for the strap even as his muscles screamed in protest.

Blood dripped into his eyes, but he could still make out the unmistakable gleam of Spanish gold inside.

A crash came from further down the tunnel, perhaps the foundations of the hotel collapsing. The chamber shook around them, and rocks rained down.

A network of cracks appeared above in the ancient ceiling, spreading quickly across the stone surface. One of the wooden support beams — centuries-old mesquite that had somehow survived the desert's dry air — groaned ominously, splintering at its center, but somehow holding. Dust and small debris sifted down through the widening fissures, coating the scattered treasure below in a fine mineral powder. It wouldn't be long until the whole thing came down.

No. He hadn't come this far to lose everything now.

Forcing his battered body to move, Barclay lurched to his knees.

His hands shook as he grabbed whatever he could reach. Reliquaries that had once held the bones of saints and chalices that had touched holy lips. Each piece represented a fortune in both historical and monetary value.

He stuffed them into the pack with none of the careful handling he'd once insisted upon. No acid-free paper, no cotton gloves, no careful cataloging of provenance. Just the desperate cramming of wealth into canvas as the chamber shook around him.

Jack shouted through the chaos. "We need to get out of here before the place comes down. Leave the rest."

But Barclay knew better than to trust the man.

He'd seen the look in Jack's eyes, the same predatory calculation he'd glimpsed in the faces of corrupt antiquities dealers and museum trustees who authenticated question-able artifacts. If he left now, Jack would return and claim everything Barclay had discovered and take all the precious gold.

His movements grew frantic.

He grabbed a heavy reliquary, its gold surface carved with scenes of torturous martyrdom.

The ground shifted beneath his feet — and Barclay clutched the reliquary to his chest as he stumbled, the weight of the thing almost too much.

He held on.

The scattered bones across the floor appeared to move in his peripheral vision, as if the mission's long-dead inhabit-ants stirred in judgment of his sins against history.

Through the blood and dust clouding his vision, Barclay caught a glimmer of gold.

A truly beautiful statue of Saint Michael lay just beyond his reach.

The archangel's open wings were portrayed in eternal flight, each feather rendered in exquisite detail by a long-dead Spanish craftsman. The piece would be worth a fortune, both to collectors and to his research about the mission's connection to indigenous tribes.

He lunged for it.

A deafening crack came from above as the ancient stone gave way.

A massive slab of ceiling rock slammed down onto Barclay's leg, pinning him to the ground. The crack of his femur breaking echoed off the chamber walls, and white-hot agony exploded through him.

Every nerve ending screamed like the suffering pains of martyrdom, as if in sympathy with those saints carved on the reliquary.

A scream tore from Barclay's throat, primal and unrestrained.

Through tears of agony, he watched Jack pick up the heavy backpack and swing it up onto his shoulder.

"Help me!" The words came out as a desperate rasp. "Please! Don't leave me here!"

Casey darted in to help him, but Jack grabbed her, yanking her back into a restraining embrace as she struggled against him.

The ground shuddered. More rocks and debris rained down.

Ancient bones from the ossuary walls broke free, clattering down around Barclay like a macabre rain.

"Please!" He tried one last time, but the others were already retreating, turning to shadows in the dust-filled air.

With a final crack, the ceiling gave way.

Centuries of sacred architecture collapsed, Barclay's scream cut short by the weight of history written in stone.

* * *

Casey struggled in Jack's iron embrace, her arms burning where he held her, his military-trained grip impossible to break.

The scent of copper filled the air. Blood and ancient metal mixing with the mineral smell of earth. Her heart hammered against her ribs as she watched the pile of broken rocks settle over where Barclay had lain.

"What have you done?" The words tore from her throat. "We could have saved him!"

She wrenched free of Jack's grip and staggered away.

He turned to face her, and the flashlight beam caught his eyes. They were as cold and dark as the desert night. The look of a man who had crossed a line and felt no remorse.

"Survival isn't a team sport. Barclay made his choice. Now you must make yours."

Casey's breath caught in her throat. His threat was clear.

As she stumbled back, she noticed a string of small red lights blinking in the darkness. Explosive charges rigged around the chamber. The whole place was going to come down, either by the force of nature, or by the hand of man.

Jack nodded up at the lights. "The countdown has already started." His voice was soft, almost gentle. "You better get out of here. All of you. Once I gather... a few things I'll be right behind you."

Casey didn't take that as good news.

She looked over at Isla and Simone. The little girl clung to her mother, fear in her eyes. Simone was clearly injured and trying to hide it from her daughter. They were all witnesses now. Jack might not have killed Barclay with his own hands, but he sure as hell let him die.

They had to get out of here. Now.

The tunnel behind was blocked. The only way out was another tunnel ahead. It looked even narrower than the last and sloped away into darkness.

Casey's chest tightened. The walls would press closer, the air would thin, the weight of earth above would—

Stop it. Focus. For Isla.

She would not lose another child.

Casey clambered over the edge of the rock pile and shone her flashlight into the tunnel. Her light wavered a little with her trembling fingers as she forced herself to breathe. The passage was tight, but it angled up.

Up meant out. Up meant away from Jack and this chamber of death. Casey forced herself to focus on that simple truth as she stared into the tunnel's throat.

She turned back and beckoned to Simone and Isla, careful to keep her movements controlled despite the trembling in her hands.

"Come on. We can go this way." The beam of her flashlight caught Isla's face, young and frightened but still trusting. Too trusting. "Stay close now."

Casey entered the tunnel first, hyper-aware of Jack behind them, picking through the treasure.

She knew his type. Men who wore civilization like a thin veneer over their primitive and dangerous core.

In the desert above, she might have a chance against him. Her knowledge of the terrain, her ability to move fast and light across open ground. But down here, in these confined spaces, her fear was a handicap, and his pure physical strength would always win.

They had to get ahead of him.

The rough stone pressed in around them, countless tons of rock suspended overhead. Ancient water courses had created treacherous dips and rises, slick with mineral deposits that could send them sprawling.

"Careful here," she called back to Simone and Isla.

Their breathing echoed in the confined space and Casey could hear Simone's controlled exhales that couldn't quite mask her pain. The shallow inhalations that suggested broken ribs. She could only hope that Simone could keep up the pace needed to stay clear of Jack.

The tunnel doglegged sharply, the walls pressing closer until Casey had to turn sideways, her back scraping against rough stone as she inched forward.

Something snagged her dress.

She couldn't move.

Her pulse skyrocketed as memories of the cave flooded back. Nausea rolled through her in waves as the walls pulsed inward with each frantic heartbeat.

Her chest seized as claustrophobia clawed at her with iron fingers, squeezing the air from her lungs.

"Are you okay, Casey?" Isla's soft voice cut through Casey's rising panic, anchoring her to the present moment.

Casey gulped, forcing herself to take slower breaths. She couldn't give in to her fear now. Not with Jack behind them.

She twisted slightly, feeling the stone's rough hardness against her spine. "Yes, I'm just caught on something."

"Stay still a minute. I can reach it." Isla's small fingers worked at the snagged fabric, and Casey felt the pressure ease a second later.

"Thank you," she called back. "Now we have to keep moving."

Behind them in the tunnel, she heard heavy footsteps. Jack would be on them soon enough.

CHAPTER 26

As they stumbled through the tunnels, Simone fought to contain her agony with each jarring step.

The pain radiated from her shoulder in vicious waves, spreading tendrils of fire across her back and down her spine. Her ribs screamed in protest with every breath, suggesting damage far worse than she'd initially considered. Each inhalation felt like dragging barbed wire through her lungs, and there was a metallic taste in her mouth.

Jack's brutal efficiency in the crypt played on repeat in her mind. The mechanical precision of his fists rising and falling, the wet sounds of impact, the way he watched Barclay disappear under the cascade of rock with cold eyes. The strength in his arms as he'd held Casey back.

Perhaps he would have been different. Perhaps they could have been happy together, if she hadn't chosen the safer path — Maxwell's wealth and status, the carefully curated life she'd built for herself and Isla. But that life was ashes now, burning above them, along with all evidence of her poisoning.

The beam of Casey's flashlight bounced erratically off the tunnel walls, transforming Isla's shadow into something fluid and strange.

Her daughter moved with grace through the darkness,

adapting to their desperate situation with a resilience that made Simone's chest ache with both pride and grief. How would this night reshape her? What scars would it leave?

Simone had killed to secure Isla's future, but now that future seemed uncertain.

Jack's footsteps echoed behind them, the sound doubling and redoubling as the stone passage played tricks with acoustics. He could be fifty feet back — or five. There was no way to tell.

He held no regard for her now, and she and her daughter were in the way of his escape. Simone was acutely aware of what that had cost Barclay.

"Mom?" Isla's voice drifted back through the darkness, tight with fear. "You need to see this."

Simone forced herself on faster, each step sending shards of agony through her injured body as she caught up to where Isla and Casey stood frozen in place.

The beam of their flashlights revealed why, and Simone's breath caught in her throat.

A chasm split the passage ahead, its depths swallowed by darkness. The void seemed to breathe as ancient air rose from below with the musty scent of centuries — limestone and stagnant water and something older, something that spoke of depths better left unexplored.

The only way across was a fragile rope bridge that spanned the void like a cobweb. Its wooden slats, grayed by time and thin air, reminded Simone of old bones.

The ropes must have been strong enough when Spanish missionaries first strung them across the abyss, sanctified by prayers that echoed through these tunnels. But time and the relentlessly dry desert air had left only decay.

Behind them, Jack's footsteps grew louder, more distinct.

"It won't hold all of us at once." Casey's voice wavered despite her obvious effort to stay positive.

Another echo of Jack's footsteps reached them. Closer now. It sounded like he was running.

A sudden blast ripped through the tunnels as Jack's explosives finished what the hotel's collapse had started.

The rock shuddered beneath them and the bridge swayed as the blast set it rocking.

Simone felt the impact through her already-damaged ribs, each breath now more ragged than the last. She clutched at the wall. There was no going back, no retreat possible through the buried crypt. The only way out was forward. Isla had to make it across.

"Go!" Simone shouted. "Don't look back, just keep moving!"

Isla took a tentative step onto the bridge. The ancient ropes creaked, and the structure dipped even with only the weight of her slight frame upon it. Simone's heart swung with it, suspended between terror and hope.

"Go, Isla," Simone called out. "I'll be right behind you."

Jack's footsteps echoed closer from the tunnel. He could only be meters away and yet Isla was only halfway across, her footsteps halting as she clung to the ropes on either side.

Casey urged Isla on, calling encouragement.

Simone still struggled for breath, her legs so weak now she could barely walk. The damage from the rocks must be radiating out to her spine.

Isla was nearly over, and Casey looked back at Simone. "You go next."

Simone shook her head. "I need a minute. You go."

Their eyes met in the dim light, and Simone knew Casey saw through her brave exterior to the pain within. The adventure guide fought her own fears down in the crushing dark, but they both had to keep going. For Isla.

Simone gave a slight nod. "Please. Help her across."

Casey turned and stepped out onto the bridge. The ropes groaned as the ancient fibers rubbed against each other, frayed — separated.

A single strand snapped, pinging off and flying into the

air. Simone could see other filaments straining as the bridge weakened with every second. It wouldn't take her weight as well as Jack's.

"Run!" she shouted.

Casey sprinted over the bridge, grabbing Isla's hand and practically dragging her across the remaining planks.

As soon as they touched solid ground, Simone launched herself forward, pushing away the pain and sprinting toward escape—

Jack darted out of the tunnel.

He grabbed her arm, his fingers digging into flesh with bruising force, and pulled her back.

Simone fought back, raking his wounded face with her nails, kicking out, writhing in his grip.

But Jack was so much stronger.

He spun her away from the ledge and slammed her into the stone wall. She dropped to the ground, gasping from the pain of her injuries as she tried to breathe. Tears welled as agony ripped through her.

"Mom!" Isla called from across the chasm. She tried to run back. But Casey held her fast, keeping the girl safe.

Jack stepped onto the bridge with the backpack of gold.

The structure dipped beneath his exaggerated weight, and the wooden planks groaned. The remaining rope fibers began to separate, each fraying cord severing a link to the other side. To her daughter.

Simone's energy ebbed away. She was done. A broken thing. The pain was too much.

"Mom, hurry! Please!" Isla's voice cut through the darkness.

She had to try. Get up. Stop Jack.

Simone forced herself up and stepped out onto the rope bridge. He turned — shoved her back — and Simone glimpsed the calculation in his eyes.

There was no love for her, and certainly none for her daughter. She couldn't let him get to Isla.

She gathered her strength and launched herself at Jack.

They went down together onto the rotting planks. The bridge bucked beneath them, swinging sideways over the void.

"You bitch!" Jack snarled, wrapping his hands around her neck as he pushed her head out over the drop.

A snap. The last rope fibers separated and tore free.

One side of the bridge gave way.

Jack let go of Simone and grabbed the wooden slats beneath him as the bridge flew across the chasm. She rolled and clung to the side rope, getting a grip—

The bridge slammed into the rock face on the other side, hanging down over the void.

Simone gasped for breath, her whole body aching from the impact as she held fast to the rope, finding footholds in what was left of the planks.

She dangled over the abyss, but unlike the movies she once acted in, there was no safety harness, no director ready to yell 'cut.'

No escape.

Her strength was fading, her injuries too much. All she wanted to do was close her eyes and rest.

"Mom!" Isla's scream echoed off the cavern walls.

Simone looked up, beyond where Jack hung above her, to see her daughter leaning over the edge, her features etched with desperation.

"Please, Mom! Climb!"

Simone somehow found a last well of strength and began pulling herself up, her bloody hands slipping on the wooden slats. Her injured ribs screamed with each movement, but she forced herself up toward Jack.

It looked like he waited for her, just slightly higher up. Perhaps he would help her. Simone felt a rush of relief. She really needed his strength now.

She looked up — reached for him.

Jack stamped down on her hand, twisting his boot on her bloody fingers. She screamed and pulled away, sliding down the slats.

He stepped down and kicked her injured shoulder, the impact sending white-hot agony through Simone's entire body. The pain was electric, all-consuming.

Her arm gave way, her fingers spasming open against her will. She was left dangling by one hand, her grip loosening with every second.

"Jack, please! Help me. Please. For what we had—"

He looked down at her, and Simone saw no trace of the man who she had once loved.

"No witnesses," he whispered, and in those words, Simone saw the threat to her daughter.

He pressed his boot down with deliberate slowness, pressing on her fingers, the bones crunching — until she slipped free.

Simone looked up, seeking one last glimpse of her daughter as she screamed.

Isla reached out toward her falling mother and Simone saw Casey pull her away from the edge, from the man who even now climbed up after them.

As Simone plummeted into the darkness, she remembered Isla's laughter as she headed out into the desert that morning — wild and free and full of joy — and wished only that her daughter could live that way always.

CHAPTER 27

CASEY PULLED ISLA AWAY from the edge as Simone's final scream echoed off the chasm walls. She hugged Isla to her chest, trying to absorb the girl's desperate sobs into her own body.

"Mommy!" Isla's cry held such raw pain that Casey felt tears well up. How could she possibly console a child who had lost both parents in one terrible night?

The sound of creaking wood came from the chasm's edge.

Gasps of effort echoed up from below as Jack hauled himself up onto solid ground. He lay there for a moment, chest heaving, as he caught his breath.

Casey held Isla tight for a beat.

They couldn't see exactly what happened below, but Jack certainly hadn't helped Simone. Perhaps he had even caused her to fall. Had they witnessed him murder two people?

Jack glanced up from where he lay — and in his eyes, Casey saw the truth. There was no time for grief.

"We have to run," Casey whispered, tightening her fingers around Isla's trembling hand. "Stay close."

Without looking back, they darted off together, plunging ahead into the tunnel system. The beam of Casey's flashlight bounced wildly as they ran, trying to put some distance between them and Jack. But there was no way to hide the echo of their footsteps. He would be after them soon enough.

"I can't..." Isla gave ragged gasps, her small body trembling with exhaustion. "I can't run anymore."

"Just a little further." Casey infused her voice with a confidence she didn't feel. "We'll find a way out."

The walls pressed closer, the ceiling dipping lower until they had to crouch. Casey's chest tightened as the space constricted. Had they taken a wrong turn? Would they hit a dead end down here with no escape?

Panic rose in Casey as Isla stumbled beside her. The girl was becoming increasingly uncoordinated, and her eyes had taken on a glassy, distant look that Casey recognized from trauma victims she'd helped rescue in the past.

Behind them, the sound of Jack's heavy footsteps coming after them.

"We have to keep going." Casey caught Isla as she stumbled again, steadying her with gentle hands. "I'm sorry, sweetie, but we have to stay ahead."

They hurried on, hand in hand, while Casey could only hope this tunnel led out of the labyrinth of rock somehow.

A sound from up ahead. Water, moving fast.

The mission records she half-remembered from guide training mentioned an underground river system, part of Death Valley's hidden hydrology.

"What's that sound?" Isla whispered, her hand tightening in Casey's grip.

"I think it's part of an ancient river system that's been flowing since the last ice age. Maybe it will help us navigate out of here."

The air changed as they raced on. It was cooler, heavy with moisture that carried a mineral scent. The rushing sound grew louder.

The tunnel opened suddenly into a cavern that their light couldn't fully illuminate, but the way their breathing echoed off distant walls told Casey they were standing in a vast space. The pressure in her chest eased as the confining walls fell away, replaced by blessed emptiness that stretched beyond their light's reach. For the first time since entering the tunnels, she could draw a full breath as her panic receded. But they weren't safe yet.

Her flashlight beam caught ripples of black water flowing past. This river had carved its path through solid rock over millennia, patient as geological time — and as uncaring.

"The water looks like ink," Isla breathed, pressing closer to Casey's side.

Casey was grateful for Isla's interest. The distraction might keep her moving a little longer. This river had to be part of Death Valley's deep aquifer system, ancient water that seeped down through fault lines and rock layers, gathering in underground reservoirs that occasionally broke through to the surface as springs. Most of it stayed hidden, flowing through lightless channels carved over millions of years.

The challenge now was how to cross it — and fast.

The cavern walls rose sheer and wet on both sides while the river churned below. The only way forward was a narrow ledge that curved along a wall, barely wide enough for walking single file.

"Look." Casey pointed at the ledge. "We can go that way."

"It looks dangerous," Isla whispered, her face pale beneath rock dust.

"We'll go slowly." Casey took her hand. "And you've only got little feet, right? Little feet, little steps. I'll go first, you follow."

Casey edged along the stone, her fingers searching for purchase against the slick stone wall.

The river rushed past just below them, its black waters swirling. She tried to keep her eyes forward, scanning for the next safe footstep. But the ledge was narrow and its surface worn smooth by millennia of underground water seeping through the rock.

Casey's foot slipped suddenly, her stomach lurching as she threw herself back against the wall, her fingers scrabbling at the wet stone as she tipped toward the churning water.

Isla's terrified gasp echoed off the cavern walls.

Casey pressed herself back against the rock, her heart thundering in her ears almost as loud as the river. She forced herself to breathe, to push back the rising panic.

"I'm okay. Just stay where you are for a moment."

Isla had pressed herself against the wall behind the ledge, her small body trembling.

A scuff of a boot on stone.

Casey glanced back to see Jack emerging from the dark tunnel.

He didn't speak. He didn't need to. He just took cold, calculated steps toward the ledge.

"Isla, we need to move faster." Casey gave a reassuring nod. "Careful now, but as quick as you can."

They shuffled forward, the ledge seeming to narrow with each step.

Water dripped from above, making the already treacherous footing even more dangerous. The sound echoed off the cavern walls, mixing with their ragged breathing and the river's constant roar.

A chunk of rock crumbled under Casey's foot without warning. She jerked back, but not before a section of the ledge broke away, leaving a gap that made the path even narrower.

The rocks tumbled into the darkness; the river's thunder swallowed the splashes.

Jack stepped onto the ledge behind them, his movements precise and predatory. In his flashlight beam, Casey could see the smile playing around his lips. He was enjoying this — enjoying their fear, their desperate attempt to escape.

"Isla, hold tight to my hand." Casey's fingers found the

girl's, squeezing gently despite her own terror. "Whatever happens, don't let go."

They were moving too fast now, fear making them reckless. As they crossed a patch of particularly slick stone, Casey felt herself slide.

She tried to compensate, but the motion only made things worse. Her center of gravity shifted.

Suddenly they were falling, Isla's scream mixing with her own as they plunged into the dark water.

The impact and the ice cold water drove the air from Casey's lungs. The current caught them immediately, spinning them in its grip like leaves in a desert windstorm. The force of it tore apart their joined hands.

Casey fought to the surface, gasping in the darkness. Her waterproof flashlight was still working, attached to her wrist with a cord, and she shone it around in desperation even as the current carried her on.

"Isla!" she shouted, trying to be heard over the river's roar. "Isla!"

A splash and gasp to her left.

Casey struck out toward the sound, her muscles already protesting against the cold. Her fingers found fabric — Isla's dress — and she pulled the girl close.

"I've got you," she gasped, trying to keep them both above water as the current swept them along. "Just hold on to me."

They shot around a bend in the underground river, the walls closing in until Casey could barely make them out in the gloom.

Jack and his flashlight beam disappeared behind them, swallowed by the darkness. His voice followed them, bouncing off the stone. "There's only one way out of here! I will find you."

The river swept them around another bend and Casey's heart seized as she saw what lay ahead.

The roof of the cave dropped sharply, meeting the water's

surface. There was no space to swim through above — they would have to go under.

Her chest tightened as memories of the cave under the Mendip Hills flooded back. Walls pressing in, air running out. Trapped.

Casey fumbled with her flashlight. The beam barely penetrated into the turbulent water, but she thought she could see a larger space beyond the wall of stone. Was that just wishful thinking, her mind seeing what she desperately needed to?

But they couldn't go back. There was no way to fight the current, and Jack was behind them somewhere in the darkness.

"We have to swim under." Casey pulled Isla close so she could hear over the water's roar. "Take a deep breath when I say and hold my hand. Don't let go, no matter what."

Isla's eyes were enormous with fear in the dim light, but she nodded. Such trust. Casey prayed she deserved it.

"Ready?" She aimed her light at the underwater gap. "Deep breath… now!"

They plunged beneath the surface together.

It was freezing. Casey fought the instinct to gasp, kicking hard with the current as they swam under the rock ledge.

Her shoulder scraped stone above, while her knees grazed the rocky bottom. The passage was brutally tight, pressing in from all sides. There was just barely enough room for she and Isla to pass through together. Her lungs burned. Her body screamed for air. Panic spiraled in her mind.

The light barely showed the way ahead through the murky water.

Then Isla's hand tugged urgently at hers, pulling upward. Casey kicked desperately to where she hoped the surface would be—

They burst into the air, gasping and spluttering in a larger cavern beyond.

"We did it," Casey managed between breaths, hugging Isla close. "You're so brave. So brave."

Casey kicked hard, angling them to the bank where rocks led up to a tunnel opening beyond. Her sodden dress dragged at her, making every movement a struggle.

"Almost there," she encouraged Isla, though her own limbs felt like lead. "Just a little further."

Her feet found rock, slippery but solid. With the last of her strength, Casey heaved them both onto a narrow shelf of stone, helping Isla scramble up beside her. They lay there for a moment, gasping, shivering. Isla's teeth chattered between gasps for air. They had to get moving before hypothermia set in.

Jack's words echoed in Casey's mind: 'Only one way out.' He knew the blueprints and had studied these tunnels. He might even be ahead of them now, waiting in the darkness.

But they couldn't stay here or death would find them with freezing fingers.

"Up we get." Casey forced herself to her feet, pulling Isla up beside her. "We need to find somewhere dry, get warmed up a bit."

They stumbled away from the river's edge, following the tunnel as it sloped gently upward.

CHAPTER 28

JUST AS CASEY THOUGHT the tunnel would never end, the passage suddenly opened up ahead. The close walls fell away as they reached a chamber that was clearly man-made.

Casey swept her light across the space. Metal glinted in the darkness, rusted rails emerging from the stone like the fossilized ribs of some ancient beast. Mining equipment lay abandoned where the last shift had left it, picks and shovels slowly becoming one with the stone as rust and mineral deposits claimed them.

The air was different — stale, metallic, with the ghost of coal smoke and dynamite. Water dripped somewhere in the darkness.

"The miners used the mission tunnels," Casey said, recalling fragments from her guide training. "These tracks will lead us to the surface."

Hope flickered in her chest. If they could follow the tracks, if they could just stay ahead of Jack long enough to find a way out—

Isla stumbled and fell to her hands and knees.

Her foot had caught on an exposed rail, sending her sprawling onto the rough-hewn floor. She sobbed in pain.

Casey dropped to her knees beside the girl, the stone floor biting through her wet clothes as her hands moved with trained efficiency to assess the injury.

Isla's ankle was twisted at a sickening angle and already beginning to swell. The skin was rapidly darkening to purple, and Casey could feel the heat of inflammation. There was no way Isla could run on it.

The sound of boots on stone, steady footfalls echoing with military precision.

Isla whimpered, her face ghost-pale in the wavering flashlight beam. Her small hand found Casey's, her fingers ice-cold and trembling.

"He's coming," she whispered.

Casey squeezed her hand gently, racing through options that grew more desperate by the second. They couldn't run, couldn't hide in this exposed chamber. The tracks led on into darkness, but with Isla's injury, they'd never outpace Jack.

The footsteps grew closer, unhurried now. Jack was taking his time, knowing he had them trapped. The bastard was probably enjoying their fear.

A minute later, Jack emerged from the tunnel, the pack of gold he still carried clinking with each step.

His flashlight beam caught them in its merciless glare, the harsh light transforming them into cornered prey.

Casey felt Isla press against her side, the girl's trembling form radiating waves of terror.

Jack gave a predatory smile. His face was a battlefield of fresh wounds — blood matted his hair where Barclay's blow had split his scalp, and angry red scratches from Simone's final desperate fight raked down his cheek. But his eyes remained cold, focused. "Nowhere left to run…"

Casey forced herself to breathe, to focus on the solid ground beneath them. She shifted position, placing herself between Jack and Isla's whimpering form.

Broken pieces of ancient rail lay around them and as he taunted them, her fingertips found a piece of sharp metal, rough with rust and age. The weight of it felt good in her hand, and she took a deep breath as she rose to her feet.

"It's over, Jack. The hotel's burning. The storm's still raging. But people will investigate. You really think you can explain the bodies?"

He laughed. "What bodies? Barclay and Simone are gone, and tragic accidents happen during a natural disaster. I'll be the hero who tried to save everyone. As long as there's no one left to say otherwise."

He took a step toward them.

Casey's grip tightened on the rail until the rust bit into her palm. Behind her, Isla's breath came in terrified gasps, as she cowered back against the wall of the mine.

Jack suddenly lunged, taking two quick steps to close the distance.

He locked his hands around Casey's throat with brutal efficiency, lifting her off her feet, his grip inexorable. He shook her, driving her back — and she dropped the rail.

She kicked uselessly at the air, searching for purchase that wasn't there.

The tunnel spun around her as Casey struggled for breath. Her lungs burned, desperate for air.

Dark spots danced at the edges of her vision, and the beam of their fallen flashlights caught dust motes that swirled in the gloom.

She clawed at Jack's arms, feeling solid muscle beneath, like attacking a stone wall. His eyes held no pity, only empty calculation.

The sound of Isla struggling to her feet penetrated Casey's fading consciousness. No, she tried to scream. Stay down. Stay safe.

Isla threw herself at Jack with desperation, her small fists pounding against his leg. "Let her go! Please, let her go!"

Jack took one hand from Casey's neck and backhanded the girl, sending her spinning across the rails in a grotesque pirouette before she crumpled to the ground, unmoving. Blood trickled from her temple.

Casey gasped for a quick breath as Jack's pressure lessened from around her throat.

Her vision sharpened as Jack studied Isla's crumpled form with professional detachment. "Maybe I'll keep her alive and take her out of here. I'll be a hero to whatever's left of her billionaire family."

His grip tightened a fraction. "She'll be traumatized, of course. Badly injured. Brain damage probably. Won't remember a thing." He gave a bitter smile. "I'll make sure of that."

His words sliced through Casey's oxygen-starved haze. He meant to deliberately hurt Isla, erase her memories of the night, and leave her even more damaged.

She could not let him hurt the girl, and she would not fail another child.

As her lungs burned for air, Casey repeated again her training instructor's mantra. Assess. Analyze. Act.

Her fumbling fingers found no weakness in Jack's grip, but close by, she saw his discarded backpack only a meter from them, the emergency flare gun still strapped to its side.

She had to act now, before unconsciousness claimed her. For Isla.

With a desperate surge of adrenaline-fueled strength, Casey drove her knee up hard, striking Jack's groin.

He grunted in pain. His grip loosened. Not much, barely a finger's width.

It was enough.

Casey twisted in his grasp. Her legs found the wall behind and she pushed off hard, throwing them both off balance.

They crashed to the ground together, the impact driving what little air remained from her lungs.

Pain exploded through her shoulder as she rolled away.

Her fingers closed around the backpack's strap, and she yanked it closer.

The flare gun's housing was cold against her palm as she

ripped it free from its holster. She was trained to protect, to rescue, not to harm.

But Jack left her no choice.

She brought the gun up with shaking hands, aiming at his face. Her vision was still blurry, her throat on fire, but the target was close enough.

Jack laughed. "Really, Casey?"

He lunged, hands reaching for the gun.

Casey's finger tightened on the trigger. The flare erupted with a deafening roar.

Phosphorus light turned the chamber bright as desert noon, burning away the shadows.

The magnesium charge caught Jack square in the face, the chemicals burning through his flesh. He screamed in agony as he staggered back, hands clawing at his ruined face as sparks bit into his skin.

The flare's light caught the labels on nearby barrels, faded warnings about explosives that had waited in the darkness. Sparks danced toward them as smoke curled from the dry wooden slats of a mining cart.

They had to get out of here before the whole place went up.

Casey scrambled to Isla and hauled the girl's limp form upright. Her muscles screamed in protest, but Jack's enraged and agonized cries drove her on.

The mine shaft tilted and swayed in their flickering flashlight beam as she half-carried, half-dragged Isla toward what she prayed was a way out.

Casey adjusted her grip, ducking down to slip Isla's arm over her shoulder while wrapping her own arm firmly around the girl's waist. This way she could take most of the weight off Isla's swollen ankle as they moved forward.

"Easy now," Casey murmured, matching her pace to Isla's limping steps. "Let me do the work."

The girl gasped a little, the pain reviving her. She rubbed her head, blood coating her hands. "Casey?"

"I'm here. We're almost safe now. Just a little further."

Jack's screams grew fainter as they stumbled on.

Around the next corner, Casey felt a breeze touch her face. She smelled desert air and the mineral scent of sand and creosote bushes.

The exit had to be close. Just a little further.

Movement ahead in the darkness made her stumble to a halt, holding Isla close. Her flashlight beam caught reflective eyes in a semicircle, low to the ground.

A pack of coyotes sheltered from the storm in the mine's entrance, their fur matted and wild. One of the largest males licked his lips, tongue showing pink against gray fur. These weren't the cautious scavengers that haunted the edge of the resort. These were feral hunters, driven inside by the storm.

The pack leader's lip curled, showing yellowed fangs. They padded down the tunnel with fluid grace, drawn by the scent of blood from Isla's head wound, sensing weakness in potential prey.

CHAPTER 29

As the pack of coyotes drew closer, Isla whimpered and pressed closer to Casey's side.

"Stay behind me," Casey whispered, her crushed throat making speech difficult.

She pushed Isla back with one hand while swinging her flashlight in a wide arc with the other.

"Hey!" she tried to shout, but it came out as a hoarse croak. She kept swinging the light, trying to make herself appear larger. "Back off!"

The coyotes paused but didn't retreat. Their eyes gleamed as they assessed the prey before them.

Behind them, the chemical stink of the phosphorus flare and the smell of smoke grew stronger.

The explosives. She'd forgotten about—

The blast hit.

Heat and pressure lifted Casey and Isla off their feet, hurling them toward the mine entrance. The coyotes fled like gray shadows.

Casey twisted in midair, trying to shield Isla from the impact. The storm's roar swallowed their screams as they burst from the tunnel mouth into chaos.

They hit sand hard enough to drive the remaining air from Casey's lungs.

For a moment, she could only lie there, stunned, Isla in her arms, as the storm raged around them. Sand stung her exposed skin, working its way under her clothes, into her nose and mouth. The wind's howl was deafening.

The remaining coyotes ran past them, vanishing into the storm. At least something had gone right, and at least they were outside.

Casey blinked grit from her eyes, trying to get her bearings.

A gust of wind shifted the swirling sand enough to reveal a familiar silhouette through the maelstrom. The hotel, or at least what remained of it.

Flames still reached toward the storm-dark sky. Surely help must be coming soon.

Casey pulled Isla closer. "We're almost safe now. Just hold on a little longer."

A roar rose above the storm.

Jack emerged from the still-smoking tunnel entrance, his skin scorched and blackened, one eye seared away. His face was a twisted mask of melted flesh and exposed bone, and his eyes blazed with rage and agony.

As the sand swirled in gusts, he caught sight of them.

He snarled and staggered in their direction.

Casey rolled up, her muscles in agony. She grabbed Isla and yanked the girl to her feet. "We have to move."

Together, they leaned into the storm, Casey supporting Isla's weight as she navigated through the gusts. The garage loomed through the maelstrom, a darker shadow in the swirling chaos of red-brown sand.

Behind them, Jack's enraged roar carried even through the wind's howl. He would not stop until he had them.

They reached the garage and Casey yanked open the side door, the hinges protesting with a shriek that was lost in the wind. She hit the automatic door button, the mechanism groaning as the main door began its slow ascent.

"Come on, come on," she muttered, releasing the buggy's restraints while the heavy door inched upward.

She lifted Isla into the passenger seat, her hands automatically checking the harness even as her eyes darted between the opening gap and Jack's approaching shadow through the curtains of blowing sand.

The keys hung on their hook. Casey's fingers shook as she jammed them into the ignition, muscle memory taking over. The engine roared to life as she positioned the buggy just inches from the rising door.

Jack burst through the side entrance, lunging for the control panel. Casey slammed her foot on the accelerator the moment the gap was wide enough. The buggy shot forward as Jack's fingers grazed the button. The door began descending, but they were already through, sand spraying in their wake as the wheels fought for purchase.

The vehicle fishtailed wildly, threatening to spin out of control. Casey wrestled with the wheel and the buggy responded to her touch, finding traction where there seemed to be none.

They shot away from Jack into the storm, the wind battering them from all sides.

A minute later, another engine started up behind them, and in the rearview mirror, a nightmare emerged from the swirling sand.

Jack hunched over the wheel of the pursuing vehicle, his burned face caught in flashes of lightning. He gunned his engine.

Casey's hands tightened on the wheel as she accelerated, almost to the edge of control.

The storm still raged, and visibility was almost zero, forcing Casey to navigate by instinct and memory.

As Isla clutched the seat beside her, Casey guided the buggy through a series of sharp turns, using the dunes' natural contours to maintain speed.

A massive impact from behind sent them lurching forward.

Jack's buggy slammed into their rear bumper.

The steering wheel tried to tear itself from Casey's grip, but she held on, her arms burning with the effort.

Another hit, harder this time.

Metal screamed against metal as Jack rammed them.

Casey jerked sideways and weaved through a gap in the dunes. Left, right, up the face of one ridge, then down the other side. Jack matched her move for move.

He slammed into them again, the impact rattling through Casey's aching body. Her fingers cramped around the steering wheel, knuckles white with strain. Isla clenched hold of the safety harness, blood from her temple wound staining her face, her eyes wide with terror.

They wouldn't last much longer out here — and Jack wouldn't stop coming.

Through the maelstrom of sand and wind, a familiar silhouette suddenly emerged. The dome of the observatory, its metal surface catching flashes of lightning that strobed through the swirling sandstorm.

Casey knew every inch of the service road up there, driving it every day in her morning ritual of solitude before the guests began their demands for the day.

But never in conditions like this, never with a child's life dependent on her skill.

The narrow track wound up the cliff face with hairpin turns and sheer drops that demanded absolute precision. Even with perfect visibility, the road was a challenge that had claimed more than one vehicle over the years. The twisted wreckage still lay scattered on the rocks below, a permanent warning to the overconfident.

Another brutal impact from behind made the buggy fishtail. Isla gasped as she clutched the roll bars, knuckles white with fear.

"Hold on." Casey wrestled with the steering wheel, fighting to maintain control as sand whipped through the open sides of the vehicle, stinging like thousands of tiny needles, forcing her to squint against the assault.

She yanked the wheel hard right, taking them up and onto the service road's first switchback.

The buggy's tires caught the edge of the track, sending a shower of stones cascading into the void beyond. The sound of their fall was lost in the howling wind, but Casey's mind filled in the long seconds before they would hit bottom.

Jack stayed glued to their tail, driving with a wild intensity, oblivious to risk.

The burns had transformed his face into something inhuman, and Casey caught glimpses of it in her mirrors, illuminated by lightning flashes. The raw, blistered flesh twisted into a grotesque mask of rage and determination.

Halfway up, on the edge of a drop-off that would send them plummeting into Badwater Basin far below, he caught them.

His buggy clipped the back wheel, the impact perfectly calculated to send them into a spin. This was no accident. He meant to send them over.

Casey's world tilted as their vehicle spun, the cliff's edge rushing toward them.

Time slowed, and she saw everything with crystalline clarity: the jagged rocks below, Isla's wide eyes, Jack's twisted smile through his cracked windshield.

The drop yawned in front of them, a thousand feet of empty air painted in strange colors by the storm, and the sharp edges of wind-carved rocks below.

The buggy's front wheels left the ground, hovering over nothing as gravity prepared to claim them.

CHAPTER 30

CASEY MOVED WITH PURE instinct, turning into the spin instead of fighting it, using their momentum to bring the buggy around.

The wheels caught traction at the last possible moment, mere inches from the edge. The engine roared as she gunned it, throwing them forward and up the next switchback.

Her heart thundered against her ribs as Casey fought to steady her breathing. Beside her, Isla was silent, in a frozen quiet that spoke of terror beyond screaming.

They were nearly at the observatory now; the structure loomed ahead like a fortress in the storm.

The wind was stronger at this elevation, buffeting their buggy with each gust. Visibility dropped to almost nothing as they crested the last rise, the swirling sand creating a curtain that hid the cliff's edge.

Perfect.

Casey's mind raced with calculations. Speed, angle, timing.

She had one chance. One opportunity to end this nightmare before Jack took them down.

Behind them, his buggy emerged from the storm like a demon from a sandstorm hell.

He gunned the engine for one last assault.

Casey yanked the wheel hard to one side, steering directly for the cliff's edge hidden behind the veil of sand. Everything hinged on split-second timing, her intimate knowledge of the landscape — and Jack's rage clouding his tactical judgment.

Casey accelerated toward the edge. Her pulse roared in her ears, louder than the storm, louder than their straining engine.

Every instinct told her to turn away from the danger, but she fought against it.

Not yet. Not yet.

Jack's buggy charged toward them. Casey's muscles coiled with tension, every sense hyperaware despite her exhaustion and injury.

She sensed the exact instant when Jack committed to his attack. The subtle shift in his engine's pitch as he floored the accelerator.

One beat. Two.

NOW.

At the last second, Casey yanked the wheel hard right, the buggy pivoting on its axis. The world spun, the vehicle's frame groaning in protest.

Jack's expression transformed from victory to horror as he realized his mistake. Too much speed, too much momentum. Too late to correct.

His buggy shot past, missing their rear fender by inches.

Casey slammed on the brakes, the tires finding just enough purchase in the loose sand to bring them to a shuddering halt.

Jack hurtled toward the void.

His desperate attempt to turn came too late. The buggy's wheels caught the rocky edge at precisely the wrong angle. The steering wheel tore from his grip, his arms pin-wheeling as the vehicle tipped.

For a moment, the buggy hung suspended, a dark silhouette against the storm-ravaged sky.

Jack's scream cut through the wind as he released his safety harness and scrambled for the side of the buggy, reaching for the cliff—

He tumbled out of sight.

Metal shrieked as the buggy bounced off the cliff face below. Distance and the storm swallowed the final crash, but Casey felt it in her bones.

She slumped against the steering wheel, trembling with the aftermath of adrenaline.

A hysterical laugh bubbled up in her raw throat. They'd made it. They were safe.

She turned to Isla, reaching to pull the girl into her arms. "It's okay now. We're—"

A roar of pure rage cut through the howling wind.

Casey spun around, scanning the cliff edge through the maelstrom of sand. As lightning split the sky, she saw Jack's fingers, bloodied and raw, clawing at the rocky edge as he dragged himself up from the abyss.

His ruined face emerged next, the phosphorus burns now caked with blood and sand, transforming his features into something barely human.

He hauled himself up with terrifying strength, his military training clear in the efficiency of his movements.

"No," Casey whispered.

Isla's hand found hers, squeezing with desperate strength. The girl's touch snapped Casey back to action.

She turned the key, willing the engine to life.

The starter whined, then died.

"Come on, come on!" Her hands shook as she tried again.

The engine coughed, spluttered, then fell silent. The damn sand had gotten into everything during their wild race.

Through the swirling red-brown haze, Jack staggered to his feet. He must be desperately injured, but rage drove him on.

His gaze locked onto them, and Casey's throat closed at the raw hatred she saw there.

She tried the engine once more. Nothing but a weak grinding sound. He would be on them too soon.

The looming bulk of the observatory lay ahead. Casey had guided countless tours there, showing off the dark skies of the desert night. She knew its layout, its quirks, its potential hiding places.

She turned to Isla. "I know it's going to hurt, but we have to run. The observatory's our only chance. I need you to be brave for just a little longer. Can you do that for me?"

Isla nodded. Her face was pale beneath the mask of red dust, but her jaw was set with determination.

"Stay close." Casey released their harnesses. "We run straight for that door, no matter what."

Another nod from Isla.

Casey threw open the buggy's door, and the full force of the storm hit them.

Sand stung every exposed inch of skin as they half-ran, half-staggered toward the observatory. The wind battered them, as if the desert itself was trying to hold them back, and the sand shifted treacherously under their feet.

Casey's arm around Isla's waist was as much for her own support as the girl's. Her throat burned with each breath. They had little energy left to fight with.

Behind them, she imagined Jack staggering forward, his every stride equal to two of theirs. An implacable force of nature, as relentless as the storm.

She didn't dare look back.

A violent gust nearly took them off their feet.

Casey stumbled, her knee twisting hard enough to send spikes of pain shooting up her leg. Isla clutched at her as Casey righted herself with a gasp.

"Almost there."

Casey could barely see the observatory, but she felt its presence ahead, pulling them forward.

"Please, I can't go on..." Isla's voice was barely a whisper against the wind's roar.

"You can." Casey pulled her closer, trying to support her wounded ankle and shield her from the worst of the flying sand. "You're the bravest person I've ever met. Just a little further. We're going to make it. I promise."

The word caught in her throat, bringing with it an echo of another promise made years ago, in the suffocating darkness of a cave under the Mendip Hills. She'd promised Eric they'd get out. Promised his parents she'd bring him home safe.

But this time would be different.

This time, she had the sky above her, not tons of crushing rock. This time, she knew exactly what she was up against. Not the impersonal threat of geology, but a man. A dangerous, desperate man, but still just a man.

The observatory door materialized out of the storm, its metal surface scoured by decades of sand-laden wind.

Casey's fingers closed around the handle, praying it wasn't locked, praying the sand hadn't jammed the mechanism.

She threw her weight against it, but the metal was unyielding beneath her bloodied palms. The handle refused to turn, sand-jammed or locked or both.

There was only one chance left. The storm shelter.

Casey grabbed Isla's hand again. "This way! There's another entrance!"

They stumbled around the curved wall of the observatory, past windows filmed with red dust.

The storm shelter's double doors appeared ahead, set at an angle into the observatory's base. Casey pulled at the handle, centuries of desert grit grinding beneath her fingers.

The doors groaned open. Stale air wafted out, carrying the musty scent of a long-disused space.

Casey ushered Isla inside, then hauled the doors shut behind them. The storm's howl became muffled, distant, though she could still feel its vibrations through the wood.

Her trembling fingers found the lock. It was old, worn, barely catching. It wouldn't hold long against a determined assault.

Casey swallowed hard, trying to quiet her ragged breathing in the sudden stillness. The darkness pressed around them, absolute and suffocating, but it wasn't like the caves below. This air carried a sharp tang of rust, old canvas, and something metallic. There must be supplies down here. Every building out here maintained basic survival stores.

She felt along the wall beside the door, where the emergency equipment should be.

Her fingers found the familiar shape of a heavy-duty flashlight. She clicked it on. The beam cut through the darkness, illuminating metal shelves lining the walls, stacked with emergency ration packs and supplies.

Isla stood in the center of the shelter, arms wrapped around herself, shivering. Desert dust coated her hair and clothes, and the blood from her temple wound seeped a little.

Casey grabbed a foil emergency blanket, the material crinkling as she tore it open and wrapped it around Isla's shoulders. "Better?"

Isla nodded, clutching the blanket tight. "Are we safe now?"

Violent banging shook the doors.

Jack's roar of rage penetrated the thick wood as he rattled it, slamming down again and again.

Casey shone the flashlight beam around the shelter, desperate for options. The space was maybe fifteen feet square, with rough concrete walls and a low ceiling crossed with pipes and conduits.

At the back, partially hidden behind a stack of supply crates, a hatch led into the observatory's lower levels.

"That way." Casey tugged Isla toward the hatch — just as the lock gave way with a crack of splintering wood.

CHAPTER 31

CASEY AND ISLA RACED for the hatch.

Behind them, the storm shelter doors burst open. Wind and sand howled in, and with them came Jack's heavy, uneven footsteps.

Casey could hear the wet rasp of his breathing. He was badly injured, but he wouldn't stop now.

She burst through the hatch into the base of the observatory's main chamber, pulling Isla up metal stairs into the grand interior.

Casey's flashlight beam caught glimpses of polished metal and precision instruments. Emergency lighting cast a dim red glow across a bank of control panels, creating more shadows than illumination.

A dramatic oversize sculpture loomed in the center of the space. The *Spirit of the Burning Land* melded ancient petroglyphs with Death Valley's natural forms, burnished copper and raw stone spiraling upward in a dance of shadow and gleam. Bighorn sheep stood forever locked in combat, while swift-footed lizards froze mid-dash across sunbaked rock, watched by the sacred human figures Timbisha Shoshone carved into canyon walls over a thousand years ago.

At the sculpture's heart, a spire of metalwork rose like an abstracted Joshua tree, its edges honed to sharp points as its branches reached out like desperate hands. Desert roses, crafted from hammered steel and copper, bloomed with edges that could draw blood, while rattlesnakes forged from twisting metal coiled through the structure.

An enormous telescope dominated the other side of the chamber, its barrel angled toward the hidden stars. Guests came here to see the Milky Way in all its glory in one of the few places left in America dark enough to witness the full majesty of the night sky.

Above it all, the massive dome loomed, its curved surface disappearing into darkness.

The space should have felt open, liberating after the confines of the storm shelter, but Casey's chest tightened at the thought of being trapped inside with Jack.

She and Isla ran on, limping, injured, as their footsteps echoed off the metal walkway. There was no way to hide the sound, and behind them, Jack's heavier tread reverberated through the structure. Slower now, but relentless.

They needed cover, something to mask their movements — and somewhere to hide.

Casey rushed to a control panel, its emergency lights blinking steadily as she slammed her palm down on the button marked OPEN.

Hydraulics whined to life, the sound echoing off the curved walls. Metal groaned against metal as the massive oculus parted, the segments of the dome sliding ponderously open. And with them came the storm.

Sand hissed against metal surfaces, driven by a howling wind. Rain followed, sporadic heavy drops that marked a change in the storm's intensity.

"We have to climb." Casey pointed to the maintenance stairway that wound up the dome's inner curve. It was meant for technicians to access the opening mechanism, but the skeletal metal structure looked barely adequate for its purpose.

It was their only option.

They were halfway up the first flight of stairs when Jack emerged onto the main floor below.

His clothes whipped in the wind that roared through the open dome, his burned and bloody face gleaming wet in the emergency lights.

He turned toward the sound of hydraulics, then his head snapped up, tracking their movement on the stairs.

"Keep climbing!" Casey pushed Isla ahead of her as they raced higher.

The metal steps grew slick with rain and treacherous under their feet. The wind pushed at them with growing strength as they ascended, making each step a battle against the elements.

The stairs hugged the dome's curve, growing steeper as they climbed, and soon they were nearly vertical, pulling themselves up as much as they used aching legs. Casey's arms trembled with exhaustion, her fingers aching where they gripped the rain-slick handrail. Isla was almost spent, her ankle swollen, her body shaking.

Jack started after them, taking the stairs two at a time despite his injuries, and the entire structure shuddered under his weight and heavy tread.

The storm grew stronger as they neared the dome's opening. Sand and rain lashed at Casey and Isla, the wind trying to tear them from their precarious perch. The emergency lights barely penetrated up here, leaving them to climb through a maelstrom of darkness split only by flashes of lightning.

Isla's foot slipped on the wet metal—

Casey lunged up, supporting her before she could fall. The movement sent pain shooting through Casey's abused muscles, but she held on, pushing Isla back onto the narrow step.

"I've got you," she gasped. "I've got you."

But for how much longer?

They were nearly at the top, where the stairs ended at a narrow maintenance platform just below the lip of the open dome. Beyond that was nothing but storm and empty air.

They had climbed as high as they could go, and still Jack came on, methodically closing the distance.

Another thunderclap boomed directly overhead and the whole observatory trembled as lightning turned the scene stark white.

Casey glimpsed the dizzying drop to the floor below, the rain driving in through the oculus, and Jack's upturned face as he ascended with terrible purpose.

The maintenance platform was their last option. Perhaps she could disconnect the stairs or something, prevent Jack from getting up to them.

Casey urged Isla up, pushing her on even as her muscles screamed. The metal stairs suddenly vibrated faster beneath her. Jack was climbing — so fast.

A hand locked around her ankle.

Casey kicked out, but his grip was unyielding.

Jack yanked hard, trying to drag Casey down. She clung to the stairs with desperate strength, but her grip was weakening. Her fingers were numb from cold, slick with rain and sweat and blood.

"Keep going, Isla! Get under the lip, as far away as you can!"

Isla hesitated a moment, then scrambled for the relative shelter where the dome's curve created a narrow overhang.

Jack reached higher and anchored his grip on Casey's belt, yanking her down, tearing her from the stairs.

He spun her around to face the dizzying drop below, one of his arms locked across her chest.

The stairs swayed beneath them as the wind howled through the gap above.

"Such a shame that you will both die here," he whispered

against her ear. "Two more unfortunate casualties of the storm."

Casey fought against his grip, but he was too strong.

The void yawned before her, a thousand feet of empty air down to the sharp spires of the sculpture below.

Movement caught Casey's eye from one side.

Isla crept down from her hiding place, clutching something in her hand — a chunk of ancient rock torn loose by the storm and hurled through the dome's opening like a gift from the desert.

Casey wanted to scream at her to stay back, to hide, to save herself, but Isla's face was set in desperate determination. She drew back her arm and threw.

The rock struck Jack's shoulder. It didn't hurt him, but he snapped his head around at the unexpected attack.

His face contorted with rage as he reached back for Isla, murder blazing in his eyes. "You little—"

The moment of divided attention was all Casey needed.

She twisted sideways, tearing out of his grip, kicking out with every ounce of strength she had left, her boot catching the back of his knee.

His leg buckled.

Jack staggered on the rain-slicked metal, his fingers clawing at empty air as lightning split the sky, illuminating his face in stark relief.

Casey met his ruined gaze for a fraction of a second — just long enough to see the dawning realization on his face, the same expression she'd seen on those who underestimated Death Valley's lethal beauty.

Then he fell, plummeting through the storm-torn air toward the *Spirit of the Burning Land* below.

The spire of the sculpture punched straight through his chest. His blood ran down the burnished copper, staining the desert stone.

CHAPTER 32

AS THE FIRST FINGERS of dawn crept across Death Valley, Casey held Isla close as they sat huddled on the steps of the observatory.

The morning light painted the sky in delicate shades of rose and gold, and the rock formations caught the early light like flames, while shadows pooled down in the valley.

The storm had finally spent itself, leaving behind an eerie stillness. The desert stretched in every direction, its harsh majesty unchanged and unchangeable by anything humans could do. Even now, the wind shifted sand over their tracks, erasing evidence of the desperate night just as it had smoothed away countless footprints before theirs.

The morning air carried the sharp mineral scent of disturbed earth, mixed with the acrid stench of burning that drifted up from below. Smoke rose in lazy spirals from the devastated remains of the hotel, twisting like spirits before dissipating into the vast sky.

"It's almost all gone," Isla whispered as they looked down upon the ruins.

Flames still licked at the twisted skeleton of warped metal and crumbling concrete. The glass dome that had been the resort's crown jewel lay shattered, its fragments scattered across the sand, already sinking beneath the surface. Within a few years, all this would be ground to powder by the endless wind.

Another section of the wall gave way with a sound like distant thunder. The carefully engineered structure collapsed in on itself, sending up a fresh plume of smoke and ash that the wind quickly caught and dispersed. Even the smoke would leave no trace, just as the tracks of prehistoric creatures that once roamed this valley had vanished beneath shifting dunes.

The wind would fill the foundations with sand, grain by patient grain, and resilient plants would take root in the ruins. The desert would reclaim it all, as it had reclaimed the Spanish mission that lay beneath. The long-dead missionaries had thought to tame this wilderness with crosses and prayers, just as Tara had tried with glass and steel. But none could stand against nature's dominion.

Ravens circled above the hotel, rising on thermals in lazy spirals. Their shadows slid over the ruins like the hands of some great clock measuring a time beyond human understanding. They had seen it all before. They would see it all again. The desert endured, timeless and absolute, while humanity's grand ambitions crumbled to dust beneath its burning sky.

Movement caught Casey's eye as a figure emerged from the smoke, backlit by flames and wreathed in swirling ash.

Even with her designer clothes in tatters and her perfect appearance ravaged by soot and blood, Tara moved with grace and confidence. Her back straight, her chin lifted in the characteristic angle that intimidated staff and impressed guests in equal measure. The gesture seemed different now, though. Less an affectation of superiority and more a declaration of survival.

Watching Tara survey the ruins of her empire, Casey remembered a staff meeting where the owner outlined her vision for the Desert Sanctuary. Harmony with the desert, sustainable luxury, and a bridge between wilderness and civilization.

There was something magnificent in Tara's defiance. Something that spoke to the same indomitable spirit that had shaped these valleys and peaks. Around her, the hotel's carefully maintained gardens had been reduced to ash, the palm trees now blackened sculptures against the dawn sky.

Tara turned slowly in place, the last of the flames reflected in her eyes, but there was no defeat in her bearing. If anything, she seemed to draw strength from the destruction, like the desert plants that bloomed more vigorously after destruction. Nature had won this round, but perhaps Tara would try again to make her mark on the desert.

More figures emerged from the smoke and debris.

Manuel, from engineering, helped a retired ecology professor navigate the treacherous wreckage. Rosa from housekeeping led a group of shell-shocked guests from the ruins, her uniform scorched but her movements still purposeful, as she cared for the wealthy visitors who usually ignored her existence.

The desert sun illuminated them all equally now, wealth and status stripped away by the democracy of survival. Designer clothes torn and blackened, expensive jewelry caked with soot, carefully maintained appearances reduced to the basic human need to keep breathing, keep moving. Keep living.

Among them, Casey spotted Grace Lin, the influencer, supporting one of the Santa Fe artists. The older woman's silver jewelry caught the morning light as they picked their way through the debris.

Grace helped the artist over a fallen beam, her own burns forgotten in her focus on helping another. All her millions of followers, all her influence, meant nothing against the desert's fury, and now they were simply two humans helping each other survive in a landscape that cared nothing for status.

The sun climbed higher, its heat already beginning to build.

The shell-shocked survivors huddled together, social barriers erased by shared trauma as a rhythmic chop-chop sound cut through the morning stillness.

Casey looked out to the west and squeezed Isla's hand. "Look, help is almost here."

The rescue helicopter swept in low over the devastated hotel, its downdraft stirring up clouds of ash and sand.

As it touched down, Casey helped Isla up and together, they began the walk back down, to safety, to help. To a new life.

Death Valley stretched out before them to the horizon. It had existed for millions of years before humans dared to build here, and would exist for millions more after everything human crumbled to dust. The salt flats shimmered like an ancient sea, and behind them, the mountains rose in layers of time made visible.

AUTHOR'S NOTE

I love deserts — or perhaps just the idea of them — and after I visited Death Valley, California, in November 2024, I knew I was ready to write a story that has been brewing for many years.

I went with Pink Jeep Tours on a day trip out of Las Vegas, but if I return, I'd like to stay in the valley to see the dark skies, which inspired the observatory that plays such a pivotal part in the story.

As ever, I have tried to keep things true to real life, but the Desert Sanctuary is not an actual place, and there is no lost mission and buried gold — or perhaps it's just not been found yet…

You can see my photos and read more at:
www.booksandtravel.page/death-valley

* * *

One of my first vivid memories is from 1983 when I flew to Malawi, in central Africa, with my brother and mum. She taught English at a university there, and we went to school in Blantyre for a while.

On the plane journey there, we were allowed to go up into the cockpit to see the captain. This was decades before 9/11, so that kind of thing was still allowed.

I remember standing there, uninterested in the dials and switches of the cockpit, but hypnotized by the Sahara desert below us. It stretched out to the horizon. It was so vast and I could see no signs of people down there.

I wanted to be out in it, and I had a sense of potential freedom that perhaps I've spent much of my life trying to recapture.

Later, in my teens, I explored the desert through books. *The Life of My Choice* by Wilfred Thesiger, as well as *Seven Pillars of Wisdom* by T.E. Lawrence, and travel books by Freya Stark and Bruce Chatwin, then *Tracks* by Robyn Davidson.

I imagined finding peace and solitude out there in the desert as a lone traveler, so I followed Robyn's footsteps to Australia. Although I wasn't alone, I camped in the outback of Western Australia and the Northern Territory and painted my skin with the ochre of red desert dust.

I've walked in the Judean desert near Qumran and slept in an eco lodge in the Negev, which inspired scenes in my thriller *Gates of Hell*. I've explored some of the Sinai desert in Egypt, before scuba diving in the Red Sea. The monastery of St Catherine is featured in my thriller *Ark of Blood*.

* * *

In terms of theme, I write often about wild nature and how insignificant we are as humans when faced with its brutal reality. I explored this theme in *Tree of Life*, and also *Blood Vintage*. Deserts perhaps take this to extremes.

I live in Somerset, England, near the Mendip Hills, and I've been caving there as well as in other areas. I've never enjoyed it much and had one experience of claustrophobia that stuck with me. If you want to read more about fascinating aspects of the underground, as well as some terrifying stories of what can happen down there, I recommend *Underland* by Robert Macfarlane, which inspired the story of the boy who died under Casey's care.

Maxwell's young blood transfusions are something the longevity-obsessed billionaires are using. Bryan Johnson is the most famous of these and you can see the treatments in the Netflix documentary *Don't Die*. I wrote about the cost of such a long life in *Tomb of Relics*.

If you're interested in the Spanish missions and how their impact continues into the present day, check out *Valley of Dry Bones*.

* * *

Practical aspects of Death Valley National Park

I love my books to be as accurate as possible, so most of the book is plausible, but as this is a novel, I took some liberties with the setting of Death Valley and what is allowed there.

Dune buggies are not driven in the park, and drones are not allowed to be used. Driving on the salt flats is also not allowed and would result in a fine. The killing of a rabbit would be illegal within the park, and there are no hunting licenses.

Thanks to Steve Hall, award-winning documentary film-maker and expert on Death Valley National Park, who read the novel and gave me valuable feedback. You can find Steve's videos on Death Valley at www.YouTube.com/stevehallDV

You can watch or listen to an episode of my Books and Travel Podcast with Steve where we discuss Death Valley at: www.booksandtravel.page/death-valley-steve-hall/

Bibliography:

Seven Pillars of Wisdom: A Triumph — T.E. Lawrence

The Explorer's Guide to Death Valley National Park, Fourth Edition — T. Scott Bryan & Betty Tucker-Bryan

The Immeasurable World: Journeys in Desert Places — William Atkins

The Life of My Choice — Wilfred Thesiger

The Songlines — Bruce Chatwin

The Southern Gates of Arabia: A Journey in the Hadhramaut — Freya Stark

Tracks: One Woman's Journey Across 1,700 Miles of Australian Outback — Robyn Davidson

Underland: A Deep Time Journey — Robert Macfarlane

ACKNOWLEDGMENTS

Thanks to Steve Hall for his expertise on Death Valley, useful feedback on the draft of the story, and his enthusiasm as a first reader.

Thanks to my editor, Kristen Tate at The Blue Garret, and my cover designer, Jane Dixon Smith at JD Smith Design. It's wonderful working with you both, as ever.

MORE BOOKS BY J.F. PENN

ARKANE Action-Adventure Thrillers

Stone of Fire #1
Crypt of Bone #2
Ark of Blood #3
One Day in Budapest #4
Day of the Vikings #5
Gates of Hell #6
One Day in New York #7
Destroyer of Worlds #8
End of Days #9
Valley of Dry Bones #10
Tree of Life #11
Tomb of Relics #12
[Stand-alone ARKANE story — Soldiers of God]
Spear of Destiny #13

Brooke and Daniel Psychological/Crime Thrillers

Desecration #1
Delirium #2
Deviance #3

Mapwalker Dark Fantasy Adventures

Map of Shadows #1
Map of Plagues #2
Map of the Impossible #3

Horror

Catacomb
Risen Gods
Blood Vintage

Short Stories

A Thousand Fiendish Angels
The Dark Queen
A Midwinter Sacrifice
Blood, Sweat, and Flame
With a Demon's Eye
Beneath the Zoo
De-extinction of the Nephilim

Travel Memoir

Pilgrimage:
Lessons Learned from Solo Walking Three Ancient Ways

More books coming soon …

You can sign up to be notified of new releases, giveaways and pre-release specials - plus, get a free ebook!

WWW.JFPENN.COM/FREE

If you loved the book and have a moment to spare, I would really appreciate a short review on the page where you bought the book.

Your help in spreading the word is gratefully appreciated and reviews make a huge difference to helping new readers find the series. Thank you!

ABOUT J.F. PENN

J.F. Penn is the Award-winning, New York Times and USA Today bestselling author of thrillers, dark fantasy, crime, horror, short stories, and travel memoir.

Jo lives in Bath, England and enjoys a nice G&T.

You can find my J.F. Penn Reading Order at:
www.jfpenn.com/readingorder

Buy books directly from me:

www.JFPennBooks.com

* * *

Sign up for your free thriller, Day of the Vikings, and receive updates from behind the scenes, research, and giveaways at:

WWW.JFPENN.COM/FREE

* * *

Connect with Jo:
www.JFPenn.com
Instagram @jfpennauthor
Facebook @jfpennauthor
X @thecreativepenn
www.BooksAndTravel.page

* * *

Love books and travel?

Check out my Books and Travel Podcast on your favorite podcast app, or find the backlist at:

www.BooksAndTravel.page/listen

For writers:

Joanna's site, www.TheCreativePenn.com empowers authors with the knowledge they need to choose their creative future. Books by Joanna Penn, as well as her award-winning show, *The Creative Penn Podcast*, provide information and inspiration on writing craft and creative business.